Tessa Buckley studied Interior Design at Chelsea College of Art. She worked in architecture and design in London until 1989, when she was forced to give up her career after developing Multiple Sclerosis. She then decided to fulfil a long held ambition to become a writer. As well as writing books about health and nutrition, and a family history blog, she now writes children's novels. *Haunted* is the second book in the *Eye Spy* series of mystery stories for older readers. She lives by the sea in Essex with her husband and son.

www.tessabuckley.com

Also by Tessa Buckley

Eye Spy

"I thoroughly enjoyed this contemporary adventure story"
Jill Murphy, best-selling author of
The Worst Witch series

"A fast-paced, exciting whodunit. A red ribbon winner"
The Wishing Shelf Book Awards.

EYE SPY II
HAUNTED

Tessa Buckley

Matador
9 Priory Business Park,
Wistow Road, Kibworth Beauchamp,
Leicestershire. LE8 0RX
Tel: (+44) 116 279 2299
Fax: (+44) 116 279 2277
Email: books@troubador.co.uk
Web: www.troubador.co.uk/matador

ISBN 978 1788032 667

British Library Cataloguing in Publication Data.
A catalogue record for this book is available from the British Library.

Printed and bound by CPI Group (UK) Ltd, Croydon, CR0 4YY
Typeset in 11pt Aldine by Troubador Publishing Ltd, Leicester, UK

Matador is an imprint of Troubador Publishing Ltd

For Lyra

Contents

1	Jimmy	1
2	How to Catch a Ghost	8
3	The Priory	14
4	An Unsettling Portrait	20
5	Mrs Liddell has a Fright	25
6	First Sighting	33
7	Spooked	40
8	The Secret Stair	46
9	Interrogating Parsons	51
10	A Missing Ring	57
11	Weighing up the Evidence	62
12	Sir John	69
13	The Celebrity Chef	75
14	Death of a Kitchen Boy	80
15	The Barbecue	85
16	The Haunting	89
17	Caught in the Act	95
18	The Poisoned Chalice	99
19	The Gofer	106
20	The Battle of the Somme	110
21	Up to No Good	114
22	A Phone Call from a Ghost	120
23	To Catch a Thief	126
24	The Golden Ball	133
25	Showdown	140
26	A Confession	146
27	Emerald Surprises Everyone	155

A Note from the Author 160

1

Jimmy

It was a Thursday, halfway through the summer term. My sister Donna and I were on our way to school, and we had just been joined by Donna's best friend Emerald. We were discussing *Ghost in Residence*, a television programme we had seen the evening before, in which various celebrities spent the night in a haunted building.

"I'd love to see a real ghost!" Donna said.

"Do you believe in ghosts, Alex?" Emerald asked. I've known Emerald forever, and she already knew the answer to that question, but she loves to tease me.

"'Course not," I said. "Nobody's ever managed to prove scientifically that ghosts exist. When they do, I'll believe in them."

"Huh!" Donna said. "Say what you like; I bet if you saw a real ghost, you'd be just as scared as anybody else."

We were still arguing about the existence of ghosts as we turned the final corner on the road to school. Suddenly, a long, sleek old-fashioned car purred past us and pulled up outside the entrance to the school. As we stood and stared, a kid with ginger hair got out of the car. He was wearing a Lea Green uniform. I couldn't see his face, but something about him was familiar. He gave a brief wave to the driver, who was wearing a peaked chauffeur's cap, before disappearing through the school gates. As the car drove off down the road, we all stared, open-mouthed.

"What's going on?" Donna asked. It was a good question. Most of the kids who go to Lea Green come from the nearby estate, and they walk or cycle to school. In Holcombe Bay, people who can afford cars like that don't send their kids to Lea Green.

Emerald giggled. "A vintage car and your own chauffeur! Perhaps he's a prince in disguise..."

"Oh, ha ha," I said. "And I suppose you're Cinderella. Come on, let's go and find out what's going on."

By the entrance gates we met up with Ryan, who was staring in the direction where the car had disappeared. He shook his head in disbelief. "That was a Rolls Royce Silver Dawn! I wonder if Dad knows who it belongs to." Ryan's dad works at the Used Car Mart, so Ryan knows loads about old cars. If he thought it was a Silver Dawn, he was probably right.

Just then the deputy head appeared and started rounding up latecomers, so we hurried inside – our first lesson was with Mr Owen, who's a stickler for timekeeping. In the rush to reach our classroom before he did, I forgot all about the boy in the chauffeur-driven car.

It was a warm day, and the classroom was stuffy. Biology isn't really my thing, and after half an hour or so of listening to Mr Owen's sing-song Welsh accent as he explained the intricacies of a plant's reproductive system, I nearly dozed off. When the bell rang for break, it was a relief to get out of the classroom and into the fresh air. As I walked into the schoolyard with Donna and Emerald, I noticed the boy with red hair who we'd seen earlier. He was standing on his own, looking a bit lost.

Now that we could see his face clearly, I realised I knew him. I turned to Donna. "Isn't that Jimmy Devlin?"

She nodded. "I remember him. He disappeared suddenly halfway through Year 6 and never came back."

"Didn't his dad run the old bakery in the High Street?" Emerald asked. "The one that's all boarded up now? So how come he's now arriving at school in a chauffeur-driven Rolls?"

Donna grinned. "Let's find out, shall we? Come on!" She strode over to where the boy was standing. "Hi, Jimmy! Remember us?"

Jimmy looked up. It took a minute for him to recognise us, then he smiled. "'Course I do. Miss Bowman used to call you *the terrible twins*."

Donna made a face. "And everyone called you Spock because of your big ears! So what have you been doing since you left Fairview Juniors?"

Jimmy glanced sideways at a group of kids hovering nearby, and jerked his head towards a less crowded part of the yard. He lowered his voice. "Let's go over there, and I'll tell you all about it." Intrigued, we followed him.

Once we'd left all the other kids behind, Donna spoke. "Come on, then. Tell us why you left Fairview so suddenly, and where you've been since."

Jimmy pulled a face. "I've been at Holcombe Academy."

We all stared at him, gobsmacked. Holcombe Academy is the private school on the other side of town. After a disastrous football match between Lea Green and Holcombe Academy, when several of the players on both sides ended up in A&E, we now do our best to steer clear of the Academy kids.

I was puzzled. "How come your parents could afford to send you there?"

Jimmy grinned. "They won the lottery!"

We all gasped. "You're kidding!" I said.

Jimmy shook his head. "I know. At first I didn't believe it either. It's true, though. It was a huge amount – enough for Mum and Dad to buy a big house, and for Dad to give up working as a baker. Then they decided that I should go to a private school."

"So why are you at Lea Green now?" I asked.

"I didn't like it there, so I got myself excluded."

I was just about to ask how he managed that, when Emerald butted in. "So where are you living now?"

"At the Priory. It's a big old house on the edge of town."

The name rang a bell. "Didn't they shoot a film there last year? It was on the local news."

"Yeah. Vintage Films used the house and grounds as a setting for *The Poisoned Chalice.* There were actors and camera crews swarming all over the place for a few weeks. It was great. I learned a lot about film-making, and my brother Harry got a part as an extra. Liddy hated it, though. She was always complaining about all the work it made for her."

"Who's Liddy?" Donna asked.

"Mrs Liddell. She's the housekeeper. Then there's Parsons – he's the chauffeur and handyman, and the butler, Furze."

"I didn't think butlers existed anymore," Donna said.

Jimmy nodded. "I used to think that too. Furze worked for the previous owner, so he sort of came with the house. So did Liddy and Parsons. By the time we moved in, Dad had bought the Rolls, because he's always wanted to own a vintage car, and he needed someone to take care of it.

I thought how weird it was that we now knew a family with servants, but Emerald was more interested in Jimmy's home. "I'd love to live in an old house like that instead of a horrible concrete tower block!" Her eyes opened wide suddenly as she asked in a hushed voice, "Is it haunted?"

Jimmy's grin faded, and he looked a bit uneasy. "Funny you should ask that. Some really strange things have been happening lately that nobody can explain."

"What kind of things?" Donna asked, glancing at me. I could tell what she was thinking. We both enjoyed solving mysteries, which was why we had started Eye Spy Investigations earlier in the year. Since then, we'd been on the lookout for a new mystery to investigate.

"Well, it started just before supper a couple of days ago," Jimmy explained. "Liddy was carrying a tray of food from the kitchen to the dining room, and when she passed the door to the cellar, she heard noises coming from behind the door."

"What sort of noises?"

"Thuds. Bangs. And…" he paused a moment before continuing, "…a child crying."

Donna frowned. "Spooky! Was the door to the cellar locked at the time?"

Jimmy nodded. "It's permanently locked because it's where Dad keeps his collection of vintage wines. They're really valuable. He only lets Furze have the key if he wants him to fetch a bottle of wine."

"Did anyone go and check out the cellar?"

"Yes. Dad did, but by the time he'd put on the light and gone down the steps, everything was quiet again. Then Liddy got upset, because Dad accused her of imagining all the noises. They had a bit of an argument, and Mum told her to take the rest of the evening off."

I wasn't sure I believed the housekeeper's story. I wondered if she had been secretly helping herself to some of the vintage wine. Then Jimmy continued, "But that's not all. The next evening, halfway through supper, all the lights in the dining room suddenly went out. And you know what the *really* odd thing was? They came on again by themselves after five minutes."

"That could have just been a power cut," I suggested.

Jimmy shrugged. "All I know is, it's all a bit weird. And the worst thing is that Dad thinks it's just me, playing tricks on everyone, and I can't prove it's not."

"Why does he think that?" Emerald asked.

"Because Harry and I used to play practical jokes on people all the time. We were always getting into trouble for it. This time, it's not me, but I don't know how to prove that to Dad."

Donna put her hand on Jimmy's arm. "Why don't

you let us help you find out what's going on at the Priory? When it comes to solving mysteries, we're experts!"

That was a bit of an exaggeration. We'd only had one case so far, after all. But then, of course, we had to tell Jimmy all about Eye Spy Investigations, and how we had set about solving the case of the missing lap dog. He was impressed, you could tell.

I thought the chance to go on a real ghost hunt was too good to miss. "Tell you what, Jimmy," I said. "See if you can persuade your mum and dad to let us sleep over at the weekend. That will give us the chance to snoop around a bit after dark and see what we can find out."

"Yes, and tonight Alex and I will do some research on ghost-hunting and try and come up with a plan of action," Donna added.

We exchanged mobile numbers so that we could keep in touch. By the time break was over, Eye Spy Investigations had its second case, and Jimmy was looking a lot more cheerful.

2

How to Catch a Ghost

When we arrived home from school, we found Nan and Dad in the kitchen. Dad was sitting at the table, doodling on a large sheet of paper. As usual, he was totally absorbed in what he was doing and didn't pay any attention to our arrival. That's typical of Dad. He's an inventor, and when he's working, he never notices what's going on around him.

A wonderful savoury smell was coming from the pan Nan was stirring at the stove. Nan works as a dinner lady at Lea Green, and she's a great cook. She turned round and nodded at us. "So how did you two get on today?"

As Donna threw her school bag down on the table and sank onto a chair, I said, "There's a new boy called Jimmy Devlin, who we used to know when we were at Fairview. He lives at The Priory."

Nan inclined her head. "Oh, aye? That's the place where they shot *The Poisoned Chalice*, isn't it? I missed it at the cinema, but I might see if I can borrow the DVD off a friend. I like historical dramas."

"Mmm... Something smells nice." Dad was back in the real world again. "I hope it's nearly ready. I'm ravenous."

I sighed with relief. Dad's moods are never predictable, and he can be really difficult to live with when his designs aren't working. I guessed his ideas were flowing well at the moment. I pointed to his doodles. "What's that, Dad? Is it a modification for Hamish?"

Hamish was the robot Dad had designed and sold to Holtech, a local technology firm and the biggest company in Holcombe Bay. He was now employed by Holtech to advise on the development of the robot – his first ever paid job. Before he sold Hamish to Holtech, it was Nan who had to pay the bills out of her wages as a dinner lady, and some cleaning jobs on the side. Now, for the first time in years, our family could afford a few luxuries. Dad was happier too. As well as a job, he now had a girlfriend: Lucy Wren, our IT teacher.

As Nan served up the meal, Dad sat back, looking smug, and announced that the doodles were part of his next and most ambitious project yet: a robot that could think for itself. "Hamish is really just a prototype," he explained. "Artificial intelligence is the future. Companies all over the world are trying to crack that one. They've got robots that can do hoovering, or remind people to take their medication, but all they can do is that one task. A robot that can make decisions for itself… now *that* could do so much more!"

"Do you think that's really possible?" I asked doubtfully.

Dad nodded. "Of course it is, Alex. And…" He paused until he was sure he had everybody's full attention "… because Holtech is committed to winning the race, they're sending me on a research trip to the States to meet some of the leading researchers in the field. I'm flying out on Sunday."

We instantly started firing questions at him. How long would he be away? Which part of the States would he be going to? Would he be meeting anyone famous? As he tried to answer them all, I felt guilty about how, until very recently, everybody – including me – had written him off as a failure.

After supper, Nan banished us upstairs to do our homework, but so much had happened that day that I found it really difficult to concentrate. Eventually I gave up and went to join Donna in her attic bedroom. She wasn't working either. We started by discussing Dad's news.

"It's difficult to think of him as a successful designer," I said. "I never realised how clever he was, because so many of the things he invented didn't work."

Donna nodded. "Remember how, every time we get into trouble at school, the Pitbull always says how we take after our father who 'never fulfilled his potential.' Next time he says that to us, we can tell him it's not true!"

The Pitbull is Mr Bull, Lea Green's Head Teacher, and he doesn't like our family. Like Donna, I wanted to prove to him that Dad wasn't a failure, but we couldn't do that yet. "No we can't. The robot project is still hush-hush, remember. Dad'll go ballistic if he finds out we've told anyone about it."

Donna sighed. "Yeah, you're right. OK, let's have a go at finding out as much as we can about ghosts and ghost-hunting. It'll give us some idea where to start."

As Donna typed 'ghosts' into the search engine on her laptop, I remembered how, in the days before Dad signed the contract with Holtech, we'd had to make do with a shared PC that Dad had cobbled together from old computers he found in a skip. Now we each had a computer and a mobile of our own.

There seemed to be several theories about who or what ghosts were. One of the most popular was the stone tape theory: '*Inanimate objects, like the walls of a building, may be able to absorb some form of energy from living beings during moments of stress. Many years later the stored energy is released to form a sort of psychic video. These moving pictures can then be triggered by someone with psychic powers.*'

"We don't know anyone with psychic powers," I pointed out.

"Yes, we do!" Donna said instantly. "Emerald!"

Emerald's grandmother is a Romany gypsy, and she's taught Emerald to read tarot cards. Before we started out on the case of the missing lap dog, Em had done a reading for us and, although there's no way I believe in fortune-telling, most of what she'd predicted did come true. However, I thought saying she had psychic powers was going a bit far, and I said so.

Donna made a face. "Well, I still think she could be useful when we're ghost-hunting. But never mind Emerald. The stone tape theory could explain ghosts, but what about strange noises or ghostly voices? That sounds more like a poltergeist to me."

She typed 'poltergeists' into the search engine and we read: '*Poltergeist phenomena, which can happen at any time of the day or night, tend to centre around a single individual, often a young person. Some researchers believe that the huge physical changes taking place in adolescence are so stressful that they cause a build-up of psychic-kinetic energy, which manifests itself as noises, smells, or moving objects.'*

Donna looked at me. "Jimmy's an adolescent. Perhaps he is the cause of all the weird things that are going on, without even knowing it."

"Maybe." Then I remembered the television documentary we'd seen the day before. "On *Ghost in Residence*, they used lots of electronic equipment to record stuff. Let's see what we can find."

After trawling through a long list of sites offering ghost-hunting weekends, I eventually reached a page that claimed to give practical advice on ghost-hunting. It was much more scientific than all the other stuff. We read how electro-magnetic field (EMF) meters could indicate the existence of paranormal activity when *'a spike in the EMF signal suggests a change in the electrical current, and thus the possible presence of a spirit.'* Night-vision cameras, which used infra-red radiation, could then be used to try and take a picture of the ghost, even at night.

Donna sighed. "It all sounds horribly expensive. How are we going to get hold of any of that stuff?"

As I continued to scroll through the list of websites, I noticed something interesting. "Hey, look at this. *'Mobile phones come with a built-in sensor that can detect electro-magnetic fields. Why not download a free EMF app to your mobile?'*"

"Brilliant. So that's one problem solved. But what do we do about a camera?"

I typed 'night-vision cameras' into the search engine.

The cheapest one advertised was £500, so buying one was out of the question..

"Maybe there'll turn out to be a perfectly rational explanation for everything that's happened, and we won't need a camera at all. For the moment, I'll just download that EMF app."

Just then, my mobile bleeped and I took it out of my pocket to check the sender. It was Jimmy. A text message appeared on the screen, and we both peered at it. It said: FRIDAY NIGHT SLEEPOVER OK.

We were all set for a ghost-hunt!

3

The Priory

Jimmy's mum and dad were so happy that he had made friends quickly at his new school that they didn't make a fuss about us sleeping over on Friday night. We arranged that we would go back to the Priory with Jimmy after school on Friday, stopping off at home on the way to pick up our gear.

As we walked through the school gates just after three o'clock on Friday afternoon, the vintage Rolls Royce was waiting outside, just as Jimmy had promised. Leaning against the bonnet, reading a copy of *The Racing Life*, was a thickset man in a chauffeur's uniform and a peaked cap. At that moment a group of boys came out of the gates, laughing and joking. When they saw the car, they stopped and stared, and one of them stretched out his hand and ran his finger over the gleaming bonnet as if to check it was real.

The chauffeur looked up from his newspaper. "Take your sticky fingers off the car, mate," he said, "or I'll make you sorry you ever laid hands on it!" The kid hurriedly stepped back onto the pavement before disappearing down the road with his friends. Donna whispered to me, "I wouldn't want to get on the wrong side of him! Look, he's got a broken nose. I bet he's been in lots of fights."

Just then Jimmy arrived, making introductions as he led us up to the Rolls. "Hiya, Alf. This is Alex and Donna. They're coming for a sleepover."

Parsons folded up his newspaper and looked us up and down. He seemed to approve of us, because he nodded at Jimmy and opened the door. "OK, mate. Hop in, all of you, and we'll get going." You could tell from his accent he wasn't local. I guessed he came from London originally.

The inside of the car was just as impressive as the exterior. The seats were covered in luxurious dark blue leather, which made a strange squashy sound as I sat down. There was a matching blue carpet on the floor, and the dashboard and the woodwork were so highly polished you could see your reflection in them. I'd never seen anything like it before. I explained to Parsons how to get to our house, and when we reached it, Donna nipped indoors to fetch our bags. While the car was parked outside, I thought I saw the lace curtains twitch at the window of the house next door. They probably wondered what was going on. We're not the sort of family whose visitors arrive in a chauffeur-driven Rolls.

Donna got back in the car, and we set off again. While the car purred through the streets of Holcombe Bay and out into the countryside beyond, Jimmy chatted to Parsons. They seemed to be on very good terms. While they discussed the favourites for the 2.40 race at Doncaster the next day, I investigated what seemed to be a pull-down picnic table behind the front seats. "I could definitely get used to this!" I whispered to Donna. She sighed with pleasure, and whispered back, "Me too!"

After a while we turned into a long tree-lined drive, which eventually opened out into a large gravelled forecourt. The car drew up in front of the Priory, and we got out. As Parsons drove the car under an archway and into a courtyard beyond, we stared up in awe at Jimmy's new home. "It's huge!" Donna breathed.

Jimmy nodded. "The bit in the middle is seven hundred years old," he informed us. "It's the original priory, where the Franciscan monks lived. The side wings were built later when it became a private house."

"You sound like a tour guide," I teased.

Jimmy went red. "History's my favourite subject, and there's a huge library here with stuff about the Priory going way back. Come on, I'll show you around."

We walked up a flight of stone steps to a front door that was black with age. It was so big that a giant could have walked through it without bumping his head. In the centre was an enormous iron knocker that Jimmy grabbed and banged against the door. The door trembled and we both jumped. "Er, Jimmy," Donna said, "don't you have a front door key?"

Jimmy shook his head. "The key to that door is as big as my hand. I don't fancy carrying that around in my pocket all day. Anyway, it's Furze's job to open the door."

As he spoke, the door creaked slowly open and a figure loomed over us. He was very tall and very thin with a slight stoop, and wore an old-fashioned black suit. His thick white hair was receding at the front and long at the back, and he had strange hooded eyes like a bird of prey. He reminded me of a huge black spider.

"Good afternoon, Master Jimmy," Furze said.

Jimmy didn't seem to be at all fazed by the butler. "Hi Furze," he said. "I've brought some friends back with me."

Furze stepped back to let us into the house. The way he looked at us made me feel nervous. "Your friends will be occupying the two bedrooms next to yours in the west wing, Master Jimmy," he said as he carefully closed the door. He turned to us. "Give me your bags and I will deposit them in your rooms." We silently handed him our bags. He definitely wasn't the sort of person you argued with. As he disappeared upstairs, Donna whispered to me, "Is he real, or did I just imagine him?"

Jimmy overheard her. "Oh, old Scrooge is OK. I found him a bit scary at first, but I'm used to him now."

"Why do you call him Scrooge?" I asked.

Jimmy grinned. "Because his name's Ebenezer, and he always looks miserable, just like the old man in that Dickens book."

As we talked, I looked around the room we were standing in. It was a vast hall with a stone-flagged floor and an elaborate carved wooden staircase in one corner, leading to the first floor. The stone walls went right up to the rafters that supported the roof, and were covered in displays of ancient weapons. At the foot of the stairs, standing like a sentry on guard, was a battered suit of armour. Jimmy saw me staring and patted the rusting armour fondly. "We call him Sir Hubert," he said. "He's almost as old as the house. Come on, we'll go and find something to eat. I'm ravenous!"

We followed Jimmy through a door underneath the staircase and down a long, gloomy stone-floored corridor where our footsteps echoed as we walked. At the far end, Jimmy pushed open another door, and we found ourselves in a large kitchen. There was a huge fireplace on one wall, an enormous wooden dresser against another wall, and a timber beamed roof just like the one in the hall. Everything else – the stove, the fridge, the dishwasher – was brand new. The only homely thing in the room was a large long-haired white cat that was curled up on a chair asleep. At the sound of our voices, it raised its head and stared at us curiously, before closing its eyes and going back to sleep again.

"That's Boss Cat," Jimmy told us. "Dad got him when Liddy complained the scullery was being invaded by rats."

There was no sign of the housekeeper. "Don't worry!" Jimmy said. "I know where she hides the cakes!" He opened a door next to the dresser, and inside was a larder the size of our spare room with rows and rows of shelves stacked with tins and packets and glass jars. Donna and I exchanged glances: the food there would have fed our family for several months. Before Dad got his new job, there had been plenty of times when our own tiny larder was almost empty. No wonder Jimmy was a bit tubbier than when we first know him.

Just as Jimmy emerged from the larder carrying a cake tin and a bumper bag of crisps, I had the strange sensation of being watched. Donna must have felt it too, because we both turned round at the same moment, just as Jimmy said, "Oh, hello Liddy. Is it OK if we have some cake?"

Mrs Liddell had moved so quietly that we hadn't heard her come into the room. I'd expected her to be large and scary like Furze, but instead she was quite short with mousy hair tied back in a pony-tail, and all her clothes were a sort of faded grey. She was the kind of person you'd never notice in a crowd.

She pursed her lips, but all she said was, "It's there to be eaten. Shall I make you some tea to go with it?" So we all sat round the huge pine table eating chocolate cake and crisps washed down with sweet milky tea, while Mrs Liddell moved around the kitchen preparing vegetables for supper and washing dishes. We couldn't talk about anything important in front of her, so as soon as we'd finished our snack, we left her to it and started our tour of the house.

4

An Unsettling Portrait

Back in the hall, I asked Jimmy to show us the cellar, where the strange noises had come from. He pointed to a door made of thick planks, blackened with age, but when we tried to open it, it was locked.

Donna frowned. "We really ought to have a look down there. Do you think you could get hold of one of the keys, Jimmy?"

Jimmy thought for a moment. "Dad keeps all the house keys on a key ring in a drawer in his desk. We might be able to get hold of them tomorrow if he goes out."

"OK," I said. "Let's leave the cellar till tomorrow. Where's the room where the lights went on and off?"

Jimmy led us through another, more modern door, and into a large room that contained a long dining table. Its surface was so highly polished that we could see our reflections in it. Around the table were twelve carved wooden chairs, and there was a gigantic matching sideboard at the other end of the room.

"Wow!" exclaimed Donna. "It's very grand! Do you eat all your meals here?"

"No. There's a smaller room, which Furze calls

the *parlour*, where we have breakfast and lunch, but we usually have supper here. This is where we were when the lights went out."

There was a large cut-glass chandelier hanging over the table and several table lamps dotted around the room. I had a quick look at the light switches and electrical sockets, and switched them on and off, but they all worked perfectly.

While I inspected the electrics, Donna was looking out of the window. She pointed to a ruined building that was just visible from the house. "What's that?" she asked Jimmy.

"That's the chapel the monks used. It doesn't look at all spooky in daylight, but I've noticed even Dad avoids it at night. Do you want a closer look?"

We went out into the garden through a side door and walked across the lawn until we reached the chapel. As we entered through a large opening at one end which must once have been the main doorway, we disturbed a couple of rooks. They flew off, cawing loudly. There was no roof left, but quite a lot of the walls were still standing, with holes where the windows had been. Jimmy was right: it was very quiet and peaceful, and with the sunlight coming through the window openings, it wasn't at all spooky.

On the far side of the chapel there was an area of rough grass and bushes divided in two by a path that led downhill towards a wooden gate. "Where does that lead?" I asked, pointing to the gate.

"There's a path on the other side that leads along the top of the cliffs and down to the caravan park near the beach," Jimmy said. "Dad keeps it locked, so we don't get dog walkers trying to cut through the grounds."

After a while we left the chapel and strolled back to the house. This time Jimmy led us in through a conservatory, which was full of plants with big blowsy flowers that gave out a sweet, sickly scent, with leaves as big as dinner plates. We were about to go into the house when we heard raised voices coming from the room beyond. We all stood still, concealed behind a particularly large potted plant, and listened. It was Mrs Liddell speaking. "If you don't mind me saying so, madam, you'd do better to have a proper sit-down dinner in the dining room. You can fit twelve people around that table. Sir John and Lady Coverly would never have considered offering guests a barbecue!"

"But I'm not Lady Coverly, and I don't want to give a dinner party!" I guessed the second voice belonged to Jimmy's mum, and she sounded cross. "Ted and I both like barbecues, and it's just the right time of year for one. If it makes extra work for you, we can hire some extra help for the evening."

"Very well, madam, as you wish. But don't blame me if something goes wrong!"

A moment later we heard a door closing as Mrs Liddell left the room. We emerged from behind the plant and followed Jimmy into the house.

In the living room we found Jimmy's mum staring at recipe books spread out on the coffee table in front of her. She looked up as we came in, and I noticed she didn't look happy. "Hello, love," she said to Jimmy. "How did you get on at school today?"

Jimmy shrugged. "It was OK. Mum, this is Alex and Donna."

Mrs Devlin smiled at us. "I'm just trying to choose some party food. Ted and I have our twentieth wedding anniversary next Saturday, and we're planning to have some friends round to celebrate."

Just then we heard the sound of voices in the hall, and a moment later a man strode into the sitting room. You could tell he was Jimmy's dad – he had the same round face and big ears, but his hair was grey not red, and the smart clothes he was wearing couldn't disguise his large stomach. Ignoring us, he gave his wife a big hug. "Not interrupting anything, am I? I've got some great news!"

Jimmy's mum smiled up at her husband. "I was just choosing some food for the party…" she began, but he didn't let her finish.

"You don't need to do that. I've engaged Martin Champion to do the catering. It's going to be a medieval banquet, and we'll have it in the garden with a spit roast and lots of genuine Tudor food. That way there will be space for more people. It will be a great evening, you'll see!"

Mrs Devlin looked worried. "But, Ted, I thought it was just going to be you and me and a few close friends." As she got up from the sofa, Mr Devlin put his arm around her shoulders and steered her towards the door. "Nonsense, Susie! This is a special day and I don't want you tiring yourself out catering. You'll love it, you wait and see." As they left the room and walked into the hall, we could still hear her protesting.

As soon as they were out of earshot, Donna turned to Jimmy. “Isn’t Martin Champion that television chef who presents *Cookery Masterclass?*”

Jimmy nodded. “Yes, that’s him. He lives near here. Dad told me he was trying to get him to do the anniversary meal, but I promised not to let on to Mum until it was settled.”

Whilst Donna and Jimmy were chatting, I was looking round at the pictures hanging on the walls. There were lots of them, but one painting in particular seemed to dominate the room. It was a portrait of an elderly man dressed in an old fashioned military uniform. Jimmy saw me staring at it. “That’s Major William Coverly. We bought the Priory from one of his descendants.”

We stood in front of the picture, examining it closely. “Isn’t he ugly?” Donna said. “I’m glad he’s not my ancestor!”

Jimmy grinned. “Mum doesn’t like him either. She says his eyes follow her around the room.”

Just then, Furze emerged from the kitchen corridor. “Dinner is served, madam,” he announced in a loud and rather pompous voice. As we followed the Devlins across the hall and into the dining room, Donna and I were struggling not to laugh.

5

Mrs Liddell has a Fright

Dinner was tomato soup followed by fish pie and vegetables, with strawberry cheesecake for pudding. Although there was loads of food, I didn't think Mrs Liddell's cheesecake was nearly as good as Nan's. Jimmy's mum waved the pudding away, saying she was on a diet, but Mr Devlin had seconds of everything. If they ate meals like this every day, I could see why they were all overweight.

Jimmy's dad seemed to be in a particularly good mood, and we soon found out why. "You're all going to have to do without me tomorrow," he announced, as he tucked into his second slice of cheesecake. "There's a classic car rally going on not far from here, and it's a great chance for me to put the Rolls through her paces!"

Mrs Devlin sighed. "I hope you don't expect me to go with you, Ted. I like the cars I travel in to be reliable, comfortable and modern. Anyway, I'm having my hair done tomorrow morning."

Mr Devlin shook his head. "You don't know what you're missing, Susie," he said, before asking Furze, who was standing silently in the background, to bring him another bottle of wine.

I was a bit disappointed that, so far, the lights had stayed firmly on. Then, just as Furze was pouring a glass of wine for Mr Devlin, there was a tremendous crash from the direction of the living room. We all jumped, and Furze almost dropped the bottle he was holding.

Mrs Devlin looked at her husband. "What on earth was that?" she asked, in a slightly trembly voice.

Mr Devlin sighed. "I'll go and find out." As he got up, he looked at Jimmy. "And if this is one of your tricks, Jimmy, you'll be in big trouble!" As he marched out of the room, closely followed by the rest of us, Jimmy was already protesting that whatever had caused the noise had nothing to do with him.

We found Jimmy's dad in the living room staring at the portrait of Major William Coverly, which lay face-down on the floor surrounded by piles of broken glass. There was a pale square on the wall where the picture had hung, but the two nails from which it had been suspended were still in place. So why had it fallen down?

Jimmy's dad was obviously wondering the same thing. He shook his head in bewilderment and turned to the butler. "You got any idea how this could have happened, Furze?"

Furze, who was doing his usual thing of hovering silently in the background, shook his head. "No, sir. It's a complete mystery to me. Shall I help you get it up off the floor?"

Together, he and Mr Devlin lifted the picture in its heavy frame and propped it against the wall, so that Mrs Liddell could sweep up the broken glass. While the adults were busy clearing up the mess, Jimmy, Donna and I slipped out of the room.

"Where can we go where nobody will overhear us?" I asked Jimmy.

He thought for a minute. "The library. I'm the only one who ever goes there."

We followed Jimmy past a room that looked like a study, and through a games room with an ancient billiard table and several dartboards. Finally we reached the library, which had tall arched windows overlooking the vast, newly-mown lawn. The walls were lined from floor to ceiling with shelves full of dusty leather-bound books, and several old-fashioned leather-covered armchairs with sagging seats were scattered around the room.

Donna sank down into one of the armchairs and stared at Jimmy. "I don't understand why your dad thinks you had anything to do with what's been happening. After all, you weren't in the locked cellar, you were with your mum and dad when the lights went out, and we were all in the dining room together when that picture fell down."

Jimmy sighed. "It's because Harry and I used to play a lot of practical jokes together. They were mainly his idea, but I tagged along and shared the blame, so now it's easy for Dad to suspect me. He doesn't believe in ghosts, so it'll take a lot to convince him that what's going on here is really supernatural."

I was curious about Jimmy's brother. "How old is Harry?" I asked. "Does he still live at home?"

Jimmy shook his head. His grin faded, and suddenly he looked sad. "Harry fell out with Dad last year, when he was eighteen. They had the most awful row about what Harry was going to do with his life, and he walked out. He hasn't been back since." Jimmy was silent for a moment, then added, "I miss him a lot, and so does Mum. She blames Dad for driving Harry away, and they argue about it a lot."

"Don't you have any idea where he might have gone?" Donna asked.

Jimmy shook his head. "Mum checked out all my aunts and uncles and cousins, but nobody has seen him. We all thought he'd come home when he ran out of money, but he never did."

I could see that talking about his missing brother upset Jimmy, so I changed the subject. "Are there any books in here about the history of the Priory?"

Jimmy nodded. He went over to the bookcase nearest the window and pulled a thick leather-covered book off a high shelf. "Look, this one is called *The Priory through the Ages.* After all those spooky things happened, I started looking for stories about the place being haunted."

"Did you find anything useful?" asked Donna.

"Not about ghosts, no, but there was lots about the history of the Priory. For instance, during the sixteenth century when it was really dangerous to be a Catholic, the owner of the Priory built a secret stair that priests could use to escape from the house into the grounds if people were searching for them."

Donna gasped. "That's really exciting! D'you have any idea where it is?"

Jimmy shook his head. "Not a clue. I thought maybe we could have a look for it tomorrow."

"Fine," I said, "but I thought we were supposed to be hunting for ghosts, not secret stairs."

Donna, who was peering at the titles of the books in the bookcase near the window, frowned at me. "Don't be such a spoilsport, Alex. We can do both." Then something caught her attention. "Look, this book is called *Myths and Legends of Holcombe Bay.* Surely that will have some ghost stories in it."

She put the book down on a small table near the window and we all crowded round. When we checked the contents page, there was a chapter about The Priory.

Over the years there have been many reported sightings of ghostly monks in the grounds of the Priory. Often these spectral figures are seen in the vicinity of the ruined chapel, and several people walking home along the cliff-top path adjacent to the chapel have claimed to hear muffled chanting, and the slow tolling of a bell.

Animals seem to be particularly sensitive to ghosts, and one incident in particular illustrates this. A man was taking a short cut through the grounds of the Priory, accompanied by his dog, and as they passed the ruined chapel the dog stopped suddenly and started growling. As the bristles on its neck stood upright, and the air chilled markedly, the man saw two hooded figures emerge from the chapel and glide towards the house. At that stage he turned and ran as fast as he could back to the cliff path, pulling the dog with him. Shortly afterwards, the footpath through the grounds, was closed to the public.

"This is all stuff that happened in the grounds," I pointed out. "Is there anything about the house being haunted?" But before we could search through the rest of the book, we became aware of loud voices in the distance.

"Someone's having an argument," Donna said. "Come on, let's see what's going on!"

We set off for the hall, where we found Mrs Liddell sitting on one of the carved wooden benches that stood on either side of the huge fireplace. Furze was standing in front of her, looking supercilious. "Don't be silly, Clarissa!" he was saying. "You must have imagined it."

Mrs Liddell looked furious. "Don't you dare tell me I'm a liar, Ebenezer Furze! I know what I saw. And what I saw was a ghost!"

Just at that moment Jimmy's mum and dad appeared in the hall. "What's going on?" Jimmy's dad demanded.

Furze curled his lip. "Mrs Liddell claims to have seen a ghost, sir."

The housekeeper glared at Furze. "I saw a shadowy figure in black monk's robes, and if that isn't a ghost, I don't know what is!"

Jimmy's mum shivered. "I told you this place was haunted, Ted," she said. "I knew it right from the start."

"Nonsense!" Mr Devlin said. "There's no such thing as ghosts. It must have been a trick of the light. Where did you see this figure?"

Mrs Liddell pulled herself together and started to explain what had happened. "I'd just loaded up the dishwasher and I was sitting down with a cup of tea. The door to the scullery was open, and as I looked towards it, this ghostly figure in a black robe drifted past the doorway."

Jimmy's dad didn't look convinced. "It must have been someone playing tricks," he said. He looked suspiciously at us. "Where were you three whilst all this was going on?"

"We've been in the library ever since supper," Jimmy replied. "Honest, Dad, this is nothing to do with us!"

Mr Devlin frowned, then shook his head. "I'm sorry if you had a fright, Mrs Liddell. Why don't you take the rest of the evening off? You too, Furze. I'll lock up tonight."

"Very well, sir," Furze said. As he left the hall, he cast a triumphant look in the direction of the housekeeper.

Once they'd both gone, Mr Devlin put his arm around his wife, who was still looking upset. "Cheer up, Susie. I'm sure there's a rational explanation for all this. I wonder if Clarissa has been at the port? I must warn Furze to keep it locked up in future." Just as they were leaving the hall, he turned back to us. "It's time you lot were in bed. And Jimmy… this had better not be one of your practical jokes. You watch your step!"

As his mum and dad left the room, Jimmy glared at their retreating backs. "I always get blamed for everything," he muttered. "It's just not fair!"

"Don't worry, Jimmy," I said as we climbed the stairs and made our way to our bedrooms. "I'm sure we can find a way to prove to your dad that all this supernatural stuff isn't your fault." Behind Jimmy's back, Donna raised her eyebrows at me. I knew what she was thinking: how on earth were we going to do that?

Donna and I had each been given a room just down the corridor from Jimmy's bedroom. When we reached my room, I beckoned the other two inside. "Come in here for a minute. We need to discuss what just happened."

Inside we found one of those ancient four-poster beds with curtains that you can close to shut yourself off from the rest of the room. We all sat down on the bed. I took my mobile out of my pocket and turned on the EDF app. "Now somebody has actually seen something that might be a ghost, we could test this out in the kitchen as soon as everyone is asleep and see if we get any positive readings."

As Jimmy nodded, Donna asked, "Can't we get the cellar key from the study whilst your dad's asleep?"

Jimmy shook his head. "He always locks the study at night, in case of burglars. We could investigate the old chapel, though. If there are any ghostly monks around, surely that's where they're most likely to be."

"OK," I said. "Let's wait in our rooms until everyone else is asleep. We'll meet up at the end of the corridor at midnight and start ghost-hunting. Right?"

The others nodded in agreement. Now we just had to wait until everybody had settled down for the night.

6

First Sighting

As I lay on the four-poster bed, fully dressed and waiting for midnight to arrive, I began to worry about all the things that could go wrong. If Mr Devlin caught us prowling around the house in the middle of the night, he'd have every right to be angry and Jimmy would be in even more trouble. The one thing I wasn't concerned about was what would happen if we came across a ghost. Like Mr Devlin, I didn't believe in ghosts. I didn't know what we'd find, but I definitely wasn't expecting anything supernatural.

I must have dozed for a bit, because I was jerked awake by the sound of the clock in the hall striking twelve. I grabbed my mobile and put it in my pocket, together with a small torch, before opening the bedroom door as quietly as I could. In the dim light from the window at the end of the corridor, I saw Donna and Jimmy waiting for me at the top of the stairs. Jimmy whispered in my ear. "Avoid the third step from the top. It creaks!"

We managed to get downstairs without making any noise, and Jimmy pointed to the door leading to the kitchen corridor. It creaked slightly as we opened it and we all froze, but the house remained quiet. After a moment we carried on down the windowless passage to the kitchen, where moonlight coming through the windows gave just enough light for us to see what we were doing. Boss Cat was asleep on the same chair he had occupied earlier. This time, he didn't stir as we crept into the room.

"Where's the scullery?" I whispered to Jimmy. He pointed to a door between the larder and the old fireplace. Donna opened the door and we peered into a small room that contained a sink, a washing machine and dryer. To our right was a door into the old stable yard. On our left was another door, which turned out to be a cupboard containing gas and electricity meters.

I got out my mobile, turned on the EMF app, and moved it slowly around the scullery. The readings remained consistently low, with no spikes. I showed it to the others. "How disappointing!" Donna said. "But I suppose it is a couple of hours since Mrs Liddell saw the ghost."

I wasn't surprised. The Priory didn't feel at all spooky to me, but I kept my thoughts to myself while I looked around the scullery and tried to work out what could have been going on. "Where do the staff sleep?" I asked Jimmy.

"Furze and Parsons each have a flat in the old stable block above the garage, and Liddy has a bedroom in the east wing."

"So if one of them wanted to frighten Mrs Liddell, they could have dressed up in a monk's habit, crept in through the back door, made her scream and then disappeared back to their flat to change out of the robes."

"Why would they want to do that?" Donna asked.

"Well, Furze certainly doesn't like her. You saw him having a go at her in the hall earlier this evening."

There didn't seem to be much more to see in the kitchen, so Jimmy unlocked the back door, using the key that was hanging on a nearby hook. "Don't talk until we're clear of the stable block," he warned us. "We don't want to wake Furze and Parsons."

Outside there was just enough moonlight to see where we were going. We followed Jimmy across the yard and round the side of the stable block into the gardens. There were soft rustlings in some of the bushes we passed, and at one point an owl hooted suddenly, startling Donna so much that she bumped into me and gave a little cry. Jimmy turned round and mouthed, "Shhh! Someone will hear us!"

I told myself the noises were just wild animals going about their business, but by the time we approached the ruined chapel my heart was beating uncomfortably fast and my stomach was starting to tie itself into knots. The others were nervous too. I could see sweat glistening on Jimmy's forehead when he glanced back at us, and Donna kept looking over her shoulder as if she was being followed.

To take my mind off my fears, I got out my mobile as soon as we were inside the ruins, but before I could turn on the app, Donna took it off me. "My turn now, little brother," she whispered. She calls me that when she needs to boost her confidence. Although we're twins, she's taller than me, as she never fails to remind me whenever she gets the chance.

Jimmy and I watched as Donna moved slowly round the remaining walls, stopping from time to time to check the screen. Eventually she rejoined us. "Any positive readings?" I asked. She shook her head.

Jimmy, who had been looking more and more uneasy, shivered suddenly. "Let's go! I've never been here at night before, and it's freaking me out!"

There didn't seem much point in staying where we were, so we all headed back across the wide lawns towards the house. We crossed the courtyard and then, as Jimmy started to pull open the back door, there was a sudden flash of movement in the room in front of us and a dark hooded figure glided across the kitchen towards the scullery. For a split second we all stopped in our tracks, transfixed by what we were seeing, until the shadowy figure was swallowed up by the darkness in the far corner of the scullery.

"What…?" I said, forgetting to lower my voice. Jimmy was so startled that he forgot to tell me to shut up, and while Donna didn't say anything, her eyes were wide with shock and she was breathing hard..

We got back into the house and closed the door, and then Jimmy and I hurried over to the meter cupboard, where the figure had disappeared. We opened the door and peered inside, but there was nothing there – only the panelled walls of the cupboard, with several meters fixed to one side wall. Jimmy's face was triumphant as he turned to me. "It just disappeared into thin air! You saw it – it must be a real ghost!"

I was pretty shaken up, and I thought he might be right, but I wasn't going to let the other two know that.

I shook my head. "Until we've ruled out every other possible explanation, nothing's definite. We've got plenty more research to do yet."

Unexpectedly, Donna backed me up. "Yes, we can carry on investigating in the morning. Right now, I'm too tired to think straight. Let's go to bed now and start again tomorrow.

She was right. There was nothing more we could do that night, so we agreed to call off the search and go to bed. We tiptoed across the wide hall where the moonlight coming through the high arched windows cast strange patterns on the floor. As we climbed the stairs I kept replaying in my mind the moment we saw the hooded figure, and wondered if it would appear again. Had I really seen my first ghost? It was a scary thought.

I was so tired that when I reached my room I threw myself down on the bed and fell instantly asleep, without bothering to change into my pyjamas. It seemed only a little while later that I was jerked awake by an ear-splitting scream. As I sat up in bed, I heard the sound of raised voices coming from somewhere nearby. I leapt out of bed and pulled open the door of my room to see what was going on. A moment later Donna's head appeared around the door of her bedroom. "What's happening?" she mouthed at me.

I shook my head as we both edged out into the corridor, trying to hear what Jimmy's mum and dad were saying. The door of a bedroom further down the corridor was slightly ajar, and I heard Mr Devlin say quite clearly, "Nonsense! You must have dreamt it!"

When she replied, Mrs Devlin's voice was shrill.

"I'm not making it up, Ted! When I came back from the bathroom I distinctly saw a hooded figure leave the corridor and disappear down the stairs."

We heard Mr Devlin snort. "Whatever you saw, Susie, it wasn't a ghost, and I'll prove it to you!" The next second the door opened and he hurried towards the stairs. He didn't notice us because it was pretty dark in the corridor and he was looking in the opposite direction. We watched him reach the head of the stairs and start to hurry down them, but then we lost sight of him as his figure was swallowed up in the shadows below. The next moment there was a terrific crash and an awful lot of swearing.

We dashed to the top of the stairs. In the hall below us there was just enough moonlight coming through the windows to see a pile of what looked like scrap metal at the base of the staircase. Then the bits of metal started to move and a muffled voice cried out, "Somebody put the damn light on!"

Donna smothered a giggle. "He must have crashed into Sir Hubert!" She began to search for a light switch. After a few seconds she found one and suddenly there was a blaze of light from the two huge chandeliers that served the hall.

As we watched, Mr Devlin hauled himself to his feet, scattering bits of metal as he did so, and trying to brush scraps of rusty chainmail off his flannel pyjamas. By that time we had been joined by Jimmy, his mum, and Mrs Liddell, who appeared suddenly and silently by my side in a dressing gown of such a pale grey that for a moment I thought she was another ghost. Mrs Devlin put her hand to her mouth. "Oh, Ted! Are you hurt? What happened?"

Mr Devlin glared up at us. "I fell over the poxy suit of armour! This house is a death trap!" He kicked the remains of Sir Hubert that lay scattered all around him on the stone floor, before climbing slowly up the stairs to join us on the landing.

By the time he reached us, he had started to see the funny side of the situation. "Come on, you lot. Back to bed now. If there were ever any ghosts around, they'll all have disappeared after that almighty racket." Then he noticed me and frowned. "Why aren't you in your night clothes?"

Too late, I realised how suspicious it looked that I wasn't wearing pyjamas like everyone else. But the hooded figure had gone downstairs, so surely he couldn't think it was me? There was no way I could have got back to the first floor unseen while he was trying to disentangle himself from the remains of Sir Hubert. "Er… I must have fallen asleep in my clothes," I stammered.

He didn't look convinced, but after narrowing his eyes at me for a moment, he shook his head. "Let's all get back to bed," he muttered, and putting his arm round his wife's shoulders, he guided her back to their bedroom.

7

Spooked

In the morning I was jerked awake by someone shaking my shoulder hard. For a moment I couldn't remember where I was, then I opened my eyes, saw the four-poster bed and realised I was at the Priory. "Wassa hurry?" I mumbled.

As Donna opened the curtains, she was already having a go at me. "Hurry up and get dressed, or you'll miss breakfast. We've got lots to do today, remember? We're going to try and investigate the cellar, and start looking for that secret stairs. And you'd better pray Jimmy's dad has forgotten he saw you fully clothed last night, or he'll be even more convinced that it's us and Jimmy pretending to be ghosts. You nearly spoiled everything."

Sometimes Donna sounds just like Nan. I turned my back on her and pretended to go back to sleep.

Once she had left the room, I got up and started to scramble into my clothes. I was curious about what they ate for breakfast in a house with a butler and a housekeeper. In the country house murder mystery I'd just been reading, they served lavish three-course breakfasts with strange-sounding dishes like devilled kidneys and kedgeree. Just thinking about those names made me feel hungry. Tucking the torch and my mobile into my pocket, I left the room and hurried downstairs.

In the hall, the remains of Sir Hubert had been cleared away. I found everybody in the room Furze called the parlour, tucking in to large plates of eggs, bacon, sausages and baked beans. I apologised for being late, and tried to hide my disappointment that there was nothing exotic about the food. As I ate my breakfast, I was waiting nervously for somebody to mention the ghostly figure Jimmy's mum had seen, but nobody said a word about it. They all seemed to be trying hard to pretend that everything was normal. Mr Devlin, who was in a very good mood, was talking to Mrs Devlin about the vintage car rally he was going to. Jimmy's mum nodded and smiled and said "Yes, dear," every time he stopped talking, but I could tell she wasn't really listening.

Eventually, when he'd polished off his plate of fried food plus several slices of toast and marmalade and a large cup of coffee, Jimmy's dad took himself off. We heard him hollering for Parsons to get the Rolls out, then shortly after that Jimmy's mum got up to go to her hair appointment. Before she left the room, she looked anxiously at Jimmy. "Now, are you three going to be alright on your own for the next few hours? Mrs Liddell will be here if you need anything before I come back."

"Don't fuss, Mum," Jimmy said. "We'll be fine." We all smiled reassuringly at her, and after waffling on for a bit longer, she finally left us alone. A few minutes later we heard the front door creak open and then shut with a massive thud as Mr and Mrs Devlin left the house. We watched from the window of the breakfast parlour as the Rolls containing Mr Devlin and Parsons drove off down the drive, followed closely by Mrs Devlin's little Nissan.

"That's a piece of luck, Mum going out as well as Dad," Jimmy said. "Now there's nobody around to ask us what we're doing."

Donna looked dubious. "What about Mrs Liddell?"

"Oh, we don't need to worry about her. She gets Saturday afternoon off anyway, but I bet that once she's finished her chores, she'll push off early to visit her daughter, and she won't come back until it's time to cook supper."

"And Furze?" I asked. "What does he do with himself?"

Jimmy glanced at his watch. "The pub in the village opens at ten thirty. He'll be off down there soon to meet his cronies.

I couldn't imagine anyone choosing to spend time with Furze, but at least it got him out of our way.

"So what are we going to do first?" Donna asked.

"We need to find the key to the cellar," Jimmy said. "I'll go and see if Dad's left his office unlocked,"

We could hear the chink of crockery and the sound of running water coming from the kitchen, which suggested that the housekeeper was still busy there, so it seemed safe to head for Mr Devlin's study. The door was shut, but not locked. Donna kept watch outside while Jimmy and I went into the room. While he rummaged around trying to find the bunch of keys, I glanced at the untidy piles of papers lying on the desk, which all seemed to be printouts of figures. I just had time to notice several copies of the *Financial Times* and the *Investor's Chronicle* lying around, when Jimmy held up a metal ring with lots of large old-fashioned keys hanging from it. "Found 'em! Come on, let's go!"

We shut the door of the office behind us and hurried down the corridor to the hall, where Jimmy put his finger to his lips. "Shhh," he said. "We need to make sure there's nobody left around." We all stood still for a moment and listened, but apart from the soft whirr of the dishwasher in the kitchen, the house was silent. We were on our own at last.

The cellar door was in a corner, underneath the staircase. It looked incredibly old, and was made of thick planks of wood fixed together with metal straps. Jimmy fitted different keys into the keyhole, one after another, trying to find the right one. Whilst he was fiddling around, I had the strange sensation that we were being watched. I told myself that was daft, because we were the only people left in the house, but I still felt uneasy. Then, as Jimmy tried the last key, we heard the lock turn. "Bingo!" he said as the door swung slowly open, revealing a flight of worn stone steps disappearing into inky darkness.

Nobody wanted to be first to go down the steps into the place where all the strange sounds had come from a few days before. Donna broke the silence. "What we need is some light. It's only scary because it's so dark." She fumbled around inside the door and eventually found a light switch. She was right: once the room below was lit up, I couldn't believe we'd all made such a fuss about going down there. I was about to pull the door shut behind us (just in case anyone returned and caught us snooping), when Jimmy grabbed my arm. "Don't do that! You can only unlock it from the hall side. We don't want to get locked in." He picked up a massive iron doorstop that was lying nearby and positioned it so the door couldn't quite shut. Then we made our way carefully down the uneven steps.

Immediately in front of us, various pieces of old furniture were lying around. Behind them was a load of metal racks that looked as if they contained Mr Devlin's collection of vintage wines. The stone walls and stone paving slabs looked very old, and there was a vaulted stone ceiling, like you see in old churches.

Donna shivered. "It's a bit chilly down here, isn't it?"

That was an understatement. The hall we had just left was warm from all the sunlight pouring in through the big windows, but in the cellar it was cold enough to have been a winter's night. "That doesn't mean anything," I said, trying to reassure myself. "Cellars are always cold, because they don't get any sunlight."

Whilst we were talking, Jimmy was investigating the bottles on the racks. "I never realised Dad had so much wine. Some of these bottles look really old. The labels are so faded you can hardly read them."

"Never mind that!" Donna said. "We're supposed to be ghost-hunting, remember? Alex, see if you can get a reading on the EMF meter."

I got out my phone and switched on the app. Just as I was checking the reading, which was normal, I felt something brush against the back of my leg. I was so startled, I cried out. Donna laughed. "Don't be silly,

Alex! It's only Boss Cat! He must have found the open door and followed us down here. Fancy being frightened of a cat!"

I felt stupid for over-reacting. Boss Cat pricked up his ears and ran off towards the other end of the cellar, which was shrouded in darkness. I guessed he was earning his keep by trying to catch some rats. I started to move around the cellar, taking EMF readings as I went. Jimmy was still hovering near the wine racks, and Donna had joined him. Then, as I approached the bottom of the stairs, the temperature suddenly went from cold to icy, and the readings on the meter spiked. Jimmy held up a dusty bottle. "Hey, Alex, look at this!" he said, just as there was an ear-splitting yowl. The cat leapt down off the top of the wine rack, knocking the bottle out of Jimmy's hands as he went, and shot off up the stairs and out of the cellar like a bolt from a crossbow. There was the sound of breaking glass as the bottle hit the floor, then the light went out and the room was plunged into darkness.

8

The Secret Stair

Things had happened so fast that we were all in shock. "Alex, where are you?" Donna called out. "I can't see a thing!"

As I tried to think straight, I remembered the torch in my pocket. "Hang on a sec," I said as I fiddled with it, but by this time I was shaking so much from cold and fear that it was really difficult to switch it on. I managed it at last, and a narrow beam of light lit up the bit of floor in front of me. As Donna and Jimmy started to move towards me, I could hear broken glass crunching underfoot. Then, just as they reached my side, there was a slight hissing sound and the electric light came on again.

We stared at each other. Jimmy gasped. "That's exactly what happened the other night! The lights went off suddenly, and then a little while later they came back on again, and nobody was anywhere near the light switches."

Donna nodded. I noticed she was shivering too. "Something spooked the cat. Animals are supposed to be more sensitive to spirits than humans. You're going to have to change your tune now, Alex, and admit that ghosts really do exist."

I was still feeling quite shaken up, but I wasn't going to tell Donna that. I shrugged. "It could have been a power cut. And anything could have spooked the cat – an extra-large rat, for instance." Donna sighed in exasperation.

"Never mind that now," said Jimmy. "There's no point in staying here. Whatever it was has gone now. Let's go back upstairs."

I pointed to the mess on the floor where the wine bottle had smashed. "We'd better clear up that first. We don't want anybody to find out we've broken a valuable bottle of wine." I walked over to the wine store and managed to kick all the broken glass under the bottom rack, where it was concealed from view.

It wasn't until all three of us were standing in the hall again that I finally managed to stop trembling. I wondered if I had the same look of shock on my face as the others had. Eventually, Donna asked, "What was the EMF reading when the lights went out, Alex?"

"It was definitely going up just before the cat got spooked."

"Then that proves it!" Jimmy said, sounding really excited. "There really is a supernatural spirit haunting the Priory!"

I nearly pointed out that there could be other explanations for everything, but I kept my mouth shut because I wasn't sure I believed that myself any more.

After locking the door and returning the keys to the desk in the study, Jimmy suggested we go and see what Mrs Liddell had left out for our lunch. My stomach was still churning gently after the fright we'd had in the cellar, but nothing – not even a suspected ghost – seemed to put Jimmy off his food.

When we reached the kitchen there was no sign of Boss Cat, but we found a plate of sandwiches, a bowl of fruit and a large bottle of fizzy drink waiting for us on the kitchen table. As we ate our lunch, we discussed all the strange things that had occurred over the last few days, trying to make sense of them all.

Donna put into words what I was thinking. "I don't get it. There are the ghostly monks, who appear in the kitchen and scullery and the upstairs corridor, and then there are all the things like lights going off and that picture falling off the wall and strange things happening in the cellar. It's as if there are two sets of spirits haunting this place."

"That's not surprising," I pointed out. "It's a very old house. Old houses often have more than one ghost"

"Oh, thanks, guys!" Jimmy said, putting down his sandwich. "I have to live here, remember, so I'd rather not have any ghosts at all, and now you say there are lots of different ones!" He looked quite upset.

"Cheer up, Jimmy," Donna said. "At least if the house really is haunted, your dad can't accuse you of causing all the strange things that are going on."

"You must have pulled some pretty spectacular stunts in the past," I said, "if he thinks you can make lights go on and off and pictures jump off walls."

Jimmy shook his head. "Harry was the one who was always playing practical jokes on people, but Dad seems to have forgotten that now. Harry got a magic set for his tenth birthday, and after that he was always making things disappear, and reappear somewhere unexpected. I enjoyed helping him, until the time when he tried that stunt where you pretend to saw somebody in half. When Mum saw my head sticking out of one side of the box, and my legs sticking out the other side, and Harry holding a real saw, she had hysterics, and Dad forbade Harry to perform magic tricks ever again."

As we sat in the sunny kitchen, listening to Jimmy describing all the pranks he got up to with Harry, it was difficult to believe that last night we had seen a ghostly figure only metres from where we were now. Donna was obviously thinking the same thing, because she left Jimmy and me chatting and disappeared into the scullery. After a few moments she called out, "Hey, come and look at this."

We joined her in the scullery, where she had opened the door of the meter cupboard. The cupboard was about two metres long and a metre wide, and all the walls were lined with ancient wood panelling covered in peeling paint. There were a couple of meters and several fuse boxes fixed to the left-hand wall.

Donna pulled open the door of the electricity fuse box. "Look!" she said. I followed her pointing finger, and saw that each fuse was labelled with the name of the room it served. I saw what she was getting at immediately. The Devlins' meter cupboard wasn't locked, so anyone who wanted to could have tampered with the fuses and caused the lights to go off and on.

Donna was frowning. "OK, so it's possible somebody master-minded the thing with the lights by taking the fuses out, but how does a real flesh-and-blood person walk into a cupboard like this and then disappear into thin air?"

Jimmy, who had been looking thoughtful, suddenly started working his way around the cupboard, tapping the panelled walls one after the other.

"What *are* you doing?" I asked.

"Listen." He tapped the left wall first, and then the middle of the back wall. "The back wall sounds different. It sounds hollow, but it shouldn't, not if the panelling is attached to a solid wall."

"I get it!" Donna said, her voice rising with excitement. "You think it's some kind of door."

"Why not?" Jimmy was running his fingers slowly over the panels, trying to find a way to open the door, if it existed. Then his thumb sank into a round indentation like a knot-hole in the wood. There was a faint click and suddenly, the whole of the back wall became a giant door that opened inwards, revealing a dark and cobwebby passage leading to a steep flight of stairs.

We had found the priest's stair!

9

Interrogating Parsons

"Wow!" Donna breathed. "Well done, Jimmy! I never thought we'd actually find it! Let's see where it goes. Alex, you've got the torch, so you can lead the way."

I took the torch out of my pocket and switched it on. The narrow beam didn't throw out much light, but it was just enough to see where we were going. I led the way as we climbed the narrow stairs slowly, in single file, trying not to slip on the uneven treads. The walls on either side of us were made of ancient stone slabs, like the hall, and there were cobwebs everywhere. They kept tickling the top of my head and catching on my clothes. At one point a spider, suspended on a silken thread, appeared right in front of my face, and I brushed it impatiently to one side. There was a damp, musty smell too, which seemed to seep out of the stone walls. After a long climb, we reached a flat surface and I stopped.

"What's the hold-up?" said Jimmy's voice from behind me.

I shone the torch from side to side. "There's just a small landing and then another wall in front of me."

"There's no point in having stairs if they don't lead

anywhere," Donna pointed out. "There must be a door somewhere ahead. See if you can find it."

I didn't see how the solid walls on either side of us could house a concealed door. The wall in front of me, however, was panelled, just like the meter cupboard, and looked more promising. Holding the torch in my left hand and directing the beam at the wall, I began to run my right hand over the panelling, just as Jimmy had done in the meter cupboard. Before long, I found a groove just big enough for my fingers, and as I pulled gently at it, the panelling began to slide to one side. As the door opened fully, I saw we were in the first floor corridor, opposite the stairs leading to the attics and near the bedroom where I'd slept the night before.

One by one, we stepped out of the dark stairwell and into the sunlit corridor. Jimmy shook his head in amazement. "How come I never discovered this before?"

Donna was examining the concealed door, which matched the carved wooden panelling covering both sides of the corridor from floor to ceiling. "Look! There's a carving here that you press to open the door. You'd never guess what it was for if you didn't know."

A lot of things fell into place in my mind as I thought about the secret stairs. The hooded monk we had seen disappear into the scullery could have escaped from us using the secret stairs, but the stairs could also have been used by the ghostly figure Jimmy's mum claimed to have seen later that night.

There was no reason to stay upstairs, so Donna and I started to make our way carefully back down the stairs, whilst Jimmy closed the secret door behind us. We had just reached the flat ground at the bottom of the stairs, when Jimmy hissed, "Listen! I can hear a car. Somebody's back!"

He was right. We could just make out faint voices and the sound of a car engine being turned off.

"Let's get out of here," Donna said. "We don't want anyone to find out what we've discovered!"

We had just arrived back in the kitchen after shutting both the secret door and the door to the meter cupboard, when Jimmy's dad came in from the yard. He seemed to be in a very good mood, and he spent a long time telling us all about the vintage car rally, and how many people had congratulated him on the Rolls.

While we were politely listening to Mr Devlin, Parsons came down the steps from his flat and disappeared into the garage. He had changed out of his chauffeur's uniform and I wondered if he was going to work on the Rolls. The secret stair had raised all sorts of questions I wanted answers to, and I guessed it would be easier to get information from Parsons than from either Furze or Mrs Liddell.

When Mr Devlin had finally disappeared indoors to look for his wife, I turned to Jimmy. "Why don't we go and talk to Parsons? We could ask him if he ever heard anything about a secret stair, and if any spooky stuff happened in the past." Jimmy nodded, and we all walked over to the garage.

The building seemed deserted when we first entered, but then Donna pointed to the two legs sticking out from underneath the Rolls. We heard the chink of metal on metal as Jimmy knelt down and peered under the car. "Hiya, Alf!" he said loudly. "Are you busy?"

There was a grunt, and the legs began to move, very slowly towards us, followed by a body in greasy blue overalls. Eventually Parsons's head appeared, and he pulled himself up into a sitting position. He glanced at his watch. "Three o'clock already, eh? Time for a break." He got to his feet and, taking a bottle of fizzy drink off a nearby shelf, took a huge swig. Then he turned to Jimmy. "OK, mate, what's up? Spill the beans to your uncle Alf."

Jimmy, who was obviously wondering where to start, hesitated before asking, "Have you heard about all the weird things that have been happening here recently?"

Parsons grinned. "Oh, yeah! I got the whole story twice: once from Ebenezer over breakfast and then again from Clarissa later. This place is turning into a right house of horrors, by all accounts, which is strange, because I don't remember any supernatural goings-on when Sir John was living here."

"So nobody saw any ghostly monks before Jimmy's family came to live here?" I asked.

Parsons shrugged. "Oh, from time to time there would be rumours about people seeing apparitions in black robes near the old chapel, but I never saw anything. In fact, I've always believed it was Sir John himself who spread the rumours, to discourage folk from cutting through his grounds on the way back from the pub." He looked sharply at Jimmy. "You know your dad suspects it's you playing tricks on everyone?"

Jimmy sighed. "I know. That's why Alex and Donna are here. They're helping me find out what's really going on. Alex – show him your card."

I dug around in my pocket and brought out one of the business cards we'd made advertising Eye Spy Investigations, and showed it to Parsons. I prayed he wouldn't laugh at us, but he just smiled broadly. "Private investigators, eh? Well, I never!"

"Alf," Donna said suddenly. "We found an old book in the library that suggested there was a secret passage somewhere in the house, an escape route for Catholic priests to use when people were hunting them down. Have either Furze or Mrs Liddell ever mentioned anything like that?"

The chauffeur scratched his head. "Can't say they have. But then I doubt if Ebenezer would tell me even if he had discovered anything. He keeps his secrets close, that one does."

I was beginning to wonder if Parsons himself had any secrets we didn't know about. I asked him how long he'd worked at the Priory, and he said he'd come down from London ten years ago in answer to Sir John's advertisement for a chauffeur. "I like messing about with cars, see. This is pretty much my ideal job, and of course the race course is just a few miles away so I can go there on my days off. I wouldn't go back to London now if you paid me."

"Were Furze and Mrs Liddell already working here when you arrived?" Donna asked.

Parsons shook his head. "There was another butler before Ebenezer, but he retired. Clarissa was here, though. Lady Coverly was ill by that time, so it was Clarissa who ran the household." He turned to Jimmy. "That's why, when your family moved in, she found it difficult to take orders from your mum. She'd got used to doing things her way."

I remembered the argument between Jimmy's mum and Mrs Liddell that we'd overheard the day before. It all made sense now.

Parsons walked round to the front of the car, poked his head under the bonnet and started to tinker with the engine. Leaving him to it, we came out of the garage into the stable-yard, where Jimmy announced that it was time for a snack. "Let's see if we can find some cake in the larder," he suggested, leading the way back to the kitchen. Unfortunately, once we got there, we found that the housekeeper had returned. When Jimmy asked if we could have some cake, she glared at us. "I don't know why you think there's any cake left when you ate it all up last night. And the Scotch eggs I was saving for lunch tomorrow! Having a midnight feast, were you?"

We stared at her. What was she talking about? "But we never went near the larder last night, Liddy," Jimmy said. "It wasn't us, honest!"

She shrugged and turned back to the sink, where she was preparing vegetables. "Suit yourself. But you can't eat what isn't there. Now, I suggest you make yourselves scarce. I'm busy."

There didn't seem to be much point in arguing with her, so we left her to it. "She's an old misery-guts!" Donna whispered in my ear as we walked out of the kitchen. "I don't know how Jimmy's mum puts up with her!"

10

A Missing Ring

By the time we reached the hall, Jimmy was fuming. "Why do I always get the blame when things go wrong round here? It's not fair!"

While Donna tried to calm Jimmy down, I glanced into the living room. Jimmy's mum was taking all the seat cushions off the sofas and armchairs and shoving her arm into all the cracks, as if she was looking for something. I watched as she searched, but she obviously didn't find what she wanted because after a while she put all the cushions back and sank down into one of the armchairs, looking tired and fed up.

I turned back to Jimmy, who was still complaining about being unfairly picked on. "Your mum doesn't look very happy. I think she's lost something."

Jimmy groaned. "Oh, not again! She's always forgetting where she's put things."

As we went into the drawing room, Jimmy's mum looked up. "Hello," she said, with a wan smile. "I hope you managed to amuse yourselves whilst we were out." As we sat down on a large, squashy sofa opposite her, we assured her that we were having a great time.

"Mum," Jimmy said, leaning forward. "What were you looking for just now?"

Mrs Devlin sighed. "It's the ring Ted bought me just after we won the lottery. He found it in an antique shop and it's really valuable. He'll be expecting me to wear it at the anniversary party. I can't think how I can have mislaid it."

"Don't worry, Mum," Jimmy said. "We'll help you look for the ring. Alex and Donna are very good at finding things that have disappeared. A few months ago they helped find a valuable missing dog."

For the second time that day, I dug our business card out of my pocket and showed it to Jimmy's mum. It was starting to look a bit dog-eared now. She smiled slightly and raised her eyebrows. "It's very kind of you to offer to help, but..."

"Don't worry," Donna broke in. "We'll be very discreet, won't we, Alex? May we ask you a few questions? For instance, when did you last see the ring?"

It seemed that last week she had got the ring out of the jewellery box where it was usually kept and had taken it to a jeweller's in town to be professionally cleaned. When she collected it a few days later, she had put it in her handbag and come home. The trouble was, she couldn't actually remember taking it out of her handbag and putting it away in the jewellery box. "That day Mrs Liddell cornered me the minute I got in the door. She wanted me to sort out some dispute she was having with Furze. It wasn't until the next day that I remembered the ring, and then I couldn't find it either in my handbag or in the jewellery box." She gave a little laugh. "I'm afraid

I'm always forgetting things, aren't I, Jimmy? Ted teases me about it a lot."

Just then Jimmy's dad came into the sitting room and saw us. "Ah, there you all are. Time for your friends to leave, Jimmy. How about I drive you home in the Rolls? There's no point in having a vintage car if you never get to drive it yourself."

So we thanked the Devlins for the sleepover, collected our overnight bags and followed Jimmy's dad out to the yard. As we all trooped through the kitchen, Mrs Liddell pointedly ignored us. We piled into the Rolls, and Mr Devlin bleeped the horn loudly before setting off down the drive and out into the countryside.

It seemed no time at all before the car ground to a halt in front of our home. As we said goodbye to Jimmy, I noticed next door's lace curtains twitching once more.

When we got indoors, Dad was busy packing for his trip to America, and Nan was fussing around, trying to make sure he didn't forget anything. Eventually he grabbed her by the shoulders and pushed her gently into an armchair. "For goodness's sake, Mum, just relax! I'm as ready as I'll ever be. Why don't you serve up supper, and Alex and Donna can tell us what it's like living at the Priory."

So whilst we ate our meal, we gave them a carefully edited version of what we'd been doing, which didn't involve spectral figures or secret stairs. We described Furze, and Mrs Liddell and Parsons, and Nan told us about Mrs Liddell's daughter Tara, who worked with her as a dinner lady at Lea Green.

After supper, Nan suggested that, as it was the

last time we would see Dad for a couple of weeks, we should all play a board game. So for the next two hours, we played Monopoly until Dad, who for once was in a really good mood, acquired so much property that the rest of us had to admit defeat. By that time I could hardly keep my eyes open because of missing so much sleep the night before, and couldn't wait to get to bed.

The next morning Nan woke us both up early so that we could say goodbye to Dad before he left. When I got down to the kitchen, he was just finishing his breakfast and Donna was bombarding him with questions about his trip.

"Are you going to see some robots that can actually think for themselves?" she asked.

Dad shook his head. "Nobody has yet come up with a robot that can make complex decisions the way humans can. That's why Holtech are sending me on a fact-finding mission. If we're going to be the first to crack that problem, we need to find out what the experts are doing."

"I hope it won't be long before you come up with a new design," Donna said. "I'm longing to be able to tell our friends what a clever dad we have!"

You could see Dad's mood suddenly change. He put down his knife and fork and stared hard at Donna. "I've told you before how crucial it is to keep my work secret. If any of Holtech's competitors get wind of what we're doing, it would be a disaster. Promise me, both of you, that you won't breathe a word about what I'm working on to anyone!"

It was the second time he'd asked us to make that

promise. We'd unintentionally let the cat out of the bag earlier in the year when we tried to get Holtech interested in his robot, Hamish, so it wasn't surprising he didn't trust us. Donna and Dad had fallen out really badly over that episode, and I knew she wouldn't want the same thing happening again.

"Don't worry, Dad," I said, trying to reassure him. "We won't say a word, will we, Donna?"

Donna, who was obviously remembering what happened last time, had gone pale. She shook her head. "No, Dad."

Dad stared hard at her for a moment, then nodded. "Good. Now, I must get going. The taxi will be here soon to take me to the airport."

After we had waved Dad off in his taxi, I wanted to discuss everything that had happened at the Priory, so as we went back indoors I suggested to Donna we should go to our den at the bottom of the garden. Nan wasn't having it. "Oh, no, you don't, my lad! You're both going to go upstairs and do your homework. And not a squeak out of either of you until it's finished and you've shown it to me."

That's typical of Nan. She thinks education is the most important thing in the world, and she never lets us forget it. As a result, we spent the rest of Sunday morning and most of the afternoon struggling with maths and history homework. Then it was time for supper, and after that we sat down with Nan to watch a television drama about a future world ruled by robots. As a result, we never did get round to talking about the ghost hunt, and what more we could do to help Jimmy.

11

Weighing up the Evidence

Monday mornings always start with Mr Bull's Year 8 assembly. Normally I don't pay much attention to whatever he's waffling on about, but that morning, he mentioned a name I recognised.

"Martin Champion?" I whispered to Jimmy, who was sitting next to me. "Isn't that the celebrity chef who's going to cook for your parents' party?" Jimmy nodded.

Mr Bull continued. "... and so Mr Champion has very kindly agreed to come and give a cookery demonstration to our Year 8 Food Technology class on Wednesday." Martin Champion is Holcombe Bay's most famous resident. and his TV programme is really popular, so there was a lot of excited chatter as the news sank in. Mr Bull raised his voice. "Quiet, please!" He glared down at us until everyone had quietened down. "I hope I can rely on all of you to be on your best behaviour on this unique occasion." He threw another frosty stare at us all before dismissing us back to our classes.

Our first lesson was maths with Mrs Kapur, who started by handing us all a test paper on quadratic equations. There were groans all round, and she banged the table with her pen. "Concentrate, please! I want to hear the cogs of your brain working!"

Things quietened down for a bit as we all struggled with the questions. Maths is not my strong point, and after a while I gave up and glanced around the room to see who else had stopped writing. Cat Williams, who has always been hopeless at maths, was whispering to her mate Jasmin, who was sitting next to her. Jasmin pointed to Donna, and they both sniggered. Donna was pretending to ignore them, but the next time Cat made a remark, Donna's head went up. "I heard that, Cat Williams!" she said, quite clearly.

"Donna Macintyre!" Mrs Kapur said. "Stop talking and get on with your work!"

Donna threw Cat a dirty look, but Emerald put a hand on her arm and I heard her whisper "Just ignore her!" After a moment, Donna started working again, and after that Cat and Jasmin left her alone.

The lesson seemed endless, but at last it was time for break. Donna and I made our way outside to our favourite spot under the chestnut tree in the yard. Donna hadn't said a word since the lesson ended, and I wanted to find out what Cat had said to upset her. Donna had fallen out with Cat a few months back when they had both been trying to impress Jason Dundy, the best-looking boy in the class. Cat had won that round, and she and Donna had been on bad terms ever since.

These days I have to be really careful what I say to Donna, because her mood can change so quickly. I complained about it to Nan the other day, and all she said was, "It's all down to hormones, Alex. Just be glad you're not a girl," which wasn't really very helpful.

In the end, curiosity got the better of me. "What did Cat say to you in class?" I blurted out.

Donna avoided the question. "I wish she and her stupid friend would just leave me alone! I hate them both!"

Before I could press her any more on what had happened earlier, we were joined by Jimmy and Emerald, and I gave up trying to get anything out of Donna. Instead I asked Jimmy if any more strange things had happened after we went home.

Jimmy shook his head. "It's all quietened down, and everything is almost back to normal. Mum's still quite jumpy, though. Every time she turns a corner, she's afraid she's going to bump into a ghost. And Furze and Mrs Liddell still aren't speaking to each other."

"So what happened at the weekend?" Emerald asked. "Come on, tell – did you see any real live ghosts?"

"There's no such thing as *live ghosts*. They're all dead. That's why they're ghosts," I said, teasing her.

Emerald gave me a friendly shove. "Very funny, Alex. Now tell me what really happened."

So we told her about the picture that fell off the wall, and the time in the cellar when the cat got spooked and the lights went out just as we got a positive EMF reading.

"But did you actually *see* anything supernatural?"

Donna nodded. "We went on a ghost hunt in the ruined chapel at midnight, but that was a waste of time really. There was nothing to see, but when we were coming back into the house, this shadowy figure in a black robe appeared and then disappeared…" Emerald gasped. "…but Alex isn't convinced it was a real ghost. It takes a lot to convince you, doesn't it, Alex?"

Emerald frowned. "You know what you need? Someone who's sensitive to troubled spirits, like the psychic in *Ghost in Residence*."

"So are you volunteering?" I was teasing her, but she took me seriously.

She stared at me. "Just because I can read tarot cards, it doesn't mean that I can summon up ghosts!"

Donna started to look interested. "No, but maybe if you can see into the future, you can also see into the past. And ghosts are just people who have lived in the past."

Emerald shivered. "It gives me a funny feeling just thinking about spirits from the past. I'm glad I don't live at the Priory."

I had a sudden thought. "I wonder if the last owners ever saw anything spooky. Are they still around, Jimmy?"

Jimmy nodded. "Lady Coverly died, but Sir John is living in a care home in the town. Dad visited him there once."

We were just digesting that bit of information when the bell rang for end of break. Before we went back inside, I promised Jimmy that we'd have a think about what to do next.

That evening, it was strange sitting down to supper without Dad. He'd never gone away for any length of time before, and although he often spent long periods in his workshop, he always turned up for supper. Nan noticed that we were unusually quiet, and tried to fill the silence by talking about her day at work.

"That Tara Liddell is a real Moaning Minnie!" she said as she handed us slices of apple pie. "If she worked a bit harder, I'd have more sympathy for her. She's been complaining all week that she hasn't got enough money for rent or food, but if she spent a little less on clothes and beauty treatments, she wouldn't have a problem. She doesn't take after her mother, that's for sure."

Donna looked up from her food. "You didn't tell us you knew Mrs Liddell, Nan."

"I only met her once," Nan said. "I did a cleaning job at the Priory after they had given a party. It's a big job running a house like that, and she's a hard worker, I'll give her that."

Nan's always banging on about how you have to work hard to get on in life. It's one of her favourite sayings. All the same, I sensed she didn't like Mrs Liddell much. "Apart from that, what did you think of her?" I asked.

"She's a bit of a bully, if you ask me. She's got that poor Mrs Devlin right under her thumb. But she's devoted to her daughter. I believe she'd do almost anything for her. Now, who's going to help me clear the table?"

When we had helped Nan out, and she had sat down in front of the television to watch her favourite soap, we disappeared upstairs to my bedroom. Once the door was firmly shut, we settled down to discuss what I had begun to think of as the Case of the Haunted Priory.

There was a lot to talk about. One thing I'd been mulling over was whether there could be a possible connection between the supernatural activity and the missing ring. "Suppose one of the staff wants to steal something," I suggested, "so they try to distract attention from what they are doing by pretending to be a ghost and making all sorts of strange things happen."

Donna frowned. "*You* may not believe that what's happening at the Priory is supernatural, but when we were in that freezing cellar and the lights went out and the cat got spooked, I was petrified!"

"You were the one who figured out how easy it was to make the lights go on and off by fiddling with the fuse box," I pointed out. "And the ghostly figure we saw in the scullery could have been someone who knew about the secret stair and used it as a hiding place. And they could have used the stair again, later that night, when Jimmy's mum saw a monk in the corridor."

Donna wasn't convinced. "Maybe… but perhaps the ring wasn't stolen at all. Even Jimmy's mum thinks she just mislaid it. If it's really lost, there's no need for anyone to pretend to be a ghost."

This time it was my turn to be doubtful. "She said the ring was a valuable antique. Sounds well worth stealing to me."

"OK, so if it was stolen, who's the most likely thief?"

"If Tara Liddell is really hard up, perhaps Mrs Liddell stole the ring to raise some cash to give to her daughter. What was it Nan said? She'd 'do almost anything for her.'"

Donna nodded. "She could also be stealing food from the house, to give to Tara, and then trying to put the blame on Jimmy."

As I thought about everything we had discussed so far, I had a nagging feeling that something didn't add up.

Then it came to me. "Donna, if Boss Cat was spooked by a spirit in the cellar, why did he remain fast asleep when the ghostly monk passed through the kitchen on Friday night? Isn't that more proof that the ghost isn't really a ghost at all?"

"Well, if it was a human being, it can't have been Furze; it wasn't tall enough for him. And it was too tall to be Mrs Liddell. That only leaves Parsons."

We were silent for a few moments while all the implications sank in. Then I remembered our conversation with Jimmy that morning. "Why don't we go and visit Sir John Coverly? He might be able to tell us more about the three staff, and any supernatural goings-on while he was at the Priory."

In the end we agreed that we would visit Sir John in his care home after school the following evening. To prevent Nan kicking up a fuss, we would tell her we were going to the library in town to do some research for a history project. I told myself it wasn't too much of a lie. After all, we *were* investigating the history of the Priory.

12

Sir John

After school on Tuesday we set off for the Pines Care Home, where Sir John Coverly lived. We caught a bus to the far side of town, and then turned off the main road into a wide tree-lined street full of big old houses. The Pines was the last house in the street.

We stood outside the two large gateposts that guarded the entrance, trying to muster up the courage to go in.

"I wonder if he'll agree to see us," Donna said as we stared at the big old house at the end of the drive. "It looks awfully posh, and he is a baronet."

I shrugged. "Well, it's worth a try. He might be able to tell us all sorts of interesting stuff about the Priory. After all, he lived there all his life."

She nodded. "OK, but we need a cover story for why we want to see him."

I remembered the story we had told Nan. "I know. We'll say we're researching local historic buildings for a history project. I bet he'll be flattered we've consulted him. Old people love talking about the past, don't they?"

Once we had agreed on tactics we walked up the drive to the front door. The whole place was very quiet; only our footsteps crunching on the gravelled drive broke the silence. We rang the bell, and after a few minutes a stern-looking woman in a pink uniform opened the door. "Yes?" she said, looking down her nose at us.

It wasn't a promising start. "Er, we'd like to see Sir John Coverly," I began. Then, as I felt Donna's foot on my toes, I shut up and let her continue.

She gave one of her brilliant smiles. "We're doing a school project on the history of the Priory, and we wondered if Sir John would very kindly agree to see us. I promise we won't tire him out, and he'd be doing us a big favour."

The woman glared at us suspiciously for a moment, and then stepped back. "You'd better come in. I'm not making any promises, mind."

We stepped inside and she shut the door behind us. We followed her across an entrance hall with a cracked marble floor and faded wallpaper, and down a long corridor. The place had a musty smell, overlaid with the scent of floor polish and overcooked vegetables. It made me feel depressed. I hoped we wouldn't have to stay there too long.

Eventually we reached a room at the back of the house overlooking the gardens, which seemed to be the residents' lounge. In one corner a couple of elderly ladies were sitting in front of a television with the sound turned down, snoring gently. In another corner a very old gentleman lay back in an armchair next to an open window. He too appeared to be snoozing. The woman in pink marched up to him and tapped him sharply on the shoulder. "Wake up, Sir John!" she said. "You've got visitors." As the old man opened his eyes, she glared at us again. "You've got half an hour. After that it will be time for his supper." Then she turned on her heel and left us to it.

Sir John was a large man with a bald head and an impressive grey moustache that curled up at the sides. He was wearing an old-fashioned three-piece suit that was stretched to breaking point over his massive stomach. He stared at us suspiciously. "Who the devil are you?"

I gulped. He was almost as scary as the Pitbull. "Um… my name is Alex Macintyre, and this is my sister Donna. It's very kind of you to see us, sir. We wondered if you could help us with our history project."

As he continued to stare at us, Donna took over. "We're looking into the history of all the old buildings in Holcombe Bay, and we are particularly interested in the Priory. We thought that as you used to live there, you might be able to give us some information about the place."

Before he could answer, Sir John started sneezing. When he eventually stopped, he dug a large handkerchief out of his pocket and blew his nose loudly. "Blasted hay fever!" he muttered. "Why do they always insist on opening the windows?"

Donna immediately walked over to the nearby window and closed it. "There, is that better, sir?"

He nodded and heaved himself into a more comfortable position, before gesturing to us to sit down. "Well, fire away, boy. What do you want to know?"

As we didn't have long, I got straight to the point. "We've found out quite a lot about the history of the Priory so far, but what's it really like to live in a house that's hundreds of years old? For instance, isn't it reputed to be haunted?"

He snorted. "Haunted? Rubbish! Never believed that stuff for a minute. Just old wives' tales, if you ask me. Pity my wife didn't feel the same, though."

He lapsed into silence, and after a moment I prompted him. "Your wife?"

"Yes, Lady Coverly never liked the place. Said it had a bad atmosphere."

"Did anything in particular happen to Lady Coverly to make her feel like that?" Donna asked. "I mean, did she actually *see* any ghosts?"

He waved a hand dismissively. "Of course not. I told you, nothing to see. But she was always complaining of hearing strange noises, and claiming things had been moved around. I told her it was just the servants, but she never believed me. That's women for you. Excuse me…" He took out his handkerchief again and proceeded to wipe his eyes vigorously.

I couldn't tell if it was hay fever that was making his eyes stream, or memories of his wife. I decided it might be time to change the subject. "Er… did you have a lot of servants when you lived at the Priory?"

"Oh, yes, when I was a child my father employed ten members of staff – six in the house and four in the gardens and stables. It's different nowadays. When the old butler left three years ago, I had the devil of a job replacing him. I was very lucky to find Furze – very lucky indeed."

I grabbed the opportunity he had given us. Furze made me feel uneasy, though I didn't know why, and I wanted to find out more about him. "I suppose you need very good references to be a butler," I said.

He nodded. "Couldn't fault his. He'd been working for some Arab prince. The man told me he thought the world of him. Can't get better than that. Not like the chauffeur. I found out later he'd got a prison record. I would have dismissed him, but by that time I was in the middle of selling up and moving here, so I let it go. Pity. He's a genius with cars."

Donna and I exchanged glances. "What was his crime?" Donna asked.

"Theft. He admitted it when I confronted him about it. Caught joyriding in a stolen car with some other young tearaways."

Just then the woman in pink came back into the room and walked over to where we were sitting. "Dinnertime, Sir John," she announced in an unnecessarily loud voice. Then she turned to us. "Time to go. I'll show you out." We barely had time to thank the old man for his help before she whisked us back through the building and out of the front door.

As we waited at the bus stop we discussed what Sir John had told us. "*Strange noises and things being moved.* That's what he said when we asked if the house was haunted. That's similar to what happened there last week. And his wife didn't like the atmosphere."

"Neither does Jimmy's mum, but that doesn't prove anything. It doesn't feel creepy to me."

Donna rolled her eyes. "Oh, come on! Don't tell me you weren't scared when the light went out in that cellar and the cat gave that bloodcurdling yowl!"

Our bus arrived just then, so I didn't have to answer. Once we were sitting down on the bus, I deliberately changed the subject. "I didn't expect the old man to say that about Parsons. Do you believe that saying, 'Once a thief, always a thief'?"

Donna frowned. "I thought if any of the servants had a dodgy past, it would be Furze, not him. Furze is always on his best behaviour in front of the Devlins, but he wasn't very nice to Mrs Liddell when she said she'd seen a ghost, was he? I think she's scared of him."

"Parsons gets on OK with Furze, though, doesn't he? Jimmy said they go down the pub together. Maybe they're partners in crime."

It was frustrating. Instead of providing us with some answers, the visit had raised a whole lot of new questions.

13

The Celebrity Chef

We didn't get a chance to speak to Jimmy the next day about our visit to Sir John, because Wednesday was the day the celebrity chef was giving his cookery demonstration. As soon as we got into school we noticed a definite buzz in the air. Lea Green is not the sort of school that normally gets visits from celebrities, and the kids who weren't lucky enough to be in Year 8 were muttering darkly about how unfair it was that they were going to miss out.

Mr Bull had explained to us that our year would be divided into two groups, and each group would get one hour with the chef. Our form was in the first group, and at eleven o'clock we joined a long line of kids waiting outside the Food Technology room. After a few minutes, the door of the room opened to reveal Mr Bull, wearing his Father Christmas face. (That's the expression he wears for parents to make him look jovial and cuddly.) I hoped he would continue to be on his best behaviour as long as Martin Champion was around.

I'd seen Martin Champion on television, but I hadn't realised just how large he was in real life. He was taller and broader than Mr Bull, and he had black hair and a beard and thick black eyebrows that almost met in the middle of his forehead. Close up, he reminded me of a picture I'd once seen of a seventeenth-century pirate.

The chef was busy laying out food and equipment on one of the workstations, helped by Miss Leski, our Food Tech teacher, who was obviously starstruck. Mr Bull ushered us into the room. Once we had all put on aprons and washed our hands, he introduced the chef and waffled on about how he had "very kindly agreed to take some hours out of his busy schedule to give us a cookery demonstration." He glanced round at us all, daring somebody to interrupt, but nobody did. "Right, Martin, over to you. The floor is yours." With a final threatening glance in our direction, he left the room.

I thought the chef looked as if he would rather be somewhere else entirely, but he summoned up a very unconvincing smile and got down to business. "Today," he announced, "I'm going to show you how to make lemon meringue pie. From time to time I'll ask for volunteers to help me. If you need to address me, you can call me Chef."

"Pompous git!" muttered someone behind me.

The Food Tech room is not very big, and there were a lot of people crammed into it. As the chef started demonstrating how to make pastry, kids at the back of the room started climbing onto tables to get a better view. By the time he had lined a baking tin with pastry and put it in the oven to cook, things were getting quite noisy, and there was a lot of pushing and shoving going on as the smaller kids tried to see what was going on. Miss Leski, who would normally have been telling everybody to shut up, was too busy gazing admiringly at Martin Champion to notice.

The chef grabbed a saucepan and set it on the hob. "Now, who's going to help me make the lemon curd?" A load of hands instantly shot up. He picked Jason Dundy and Cat Williams, and I saw Cat smirk as she passed Donna on the way to join Martin Champion. Donna pretended not to notice.

While Jason beat egg yolks and Cat squeezed lemons, looking very pleased with herself, the chef was heating something in a saucepan on the hob. When all the ingredients were finally bubbling away and Jason and Cat had rejoined the rest of us, he asked for another volunteer to make the meringue. Just then a boy behind me gave a shove, and as I stepped forward to get out of his way, the chef beckoned to me. Too late, I realised he thought I had volunteered. As I joined him by the cooking station, he looked more like a pirate than ever.

"I need you to do some whisking," he said, handing me a bowl of egg white and an electric whisk. With him breathing down my neck and all eyes on me, I just wanted to get it over with, so I wasn't paying much attention to what he was saying to me. As I plunged the whisk into the sticky mixture and switched it on, to my horror, egg white spurted out in all directions. Amid hoots of laughter, I hurriedly switched off the whisk.

The chef glared at me, then pointed to the pool of sticky liquid on the floor. "Look what you've done, you stupid boy! Didn't you hear me tell you to switch it on *before* you put it in the bowl?"

"Sorry, Chef," I muttered, before hurrying back to join the other kids.

While Miss Leski rushed off to look for a mop, the chef, looking grim-faced, went to find some more eggs. Then a voice from the back of the room piped up, "I can smell burning!" Too late, Martin Champion noticed the pan he had left on the hob, from which smoke was rising. Unfortunately, as he dashed to the hob to remove the pan, he skidded on the pool of sticky egg white, lost his balance and ended up on his back on the floor. The next moment the fire alarm went off.

Twenty minutes later, the whole school was lined up in the yard, and a thunderous-looking Mr Bull addressed us. "Due to the stupidity of some Year 8 pupils, who don't know how to behave, the whole school day has been disrupted, and Martin Champion is unfortunately no longer able to give a second cookery demonstration." A wail went up from all the kids who had lost out. Then, just as he was opening his mouth to begin another list of complaints about our behaviour, we heard the fire alarm go off for the second time that day.

Miss Leski, who was standing nearby, went pale. "Oh no! The pie's still in the oven!" she muttered, before running back inside the building. Mr Bull shook his head in disbelief.

I was praying the chef hadn't identified me as the boy who caused the fiasco at the cookery demo, but I was out of luck. As we waited for the all-clear to go back inside, Mr Bull's eyes roved slowly over everyone in our class until finally they rested on me. "You, boy," he barked, pointing at me. "Over here!" Reluctantly, I walked over to where he was standing. He glared at me. "I understand it was your clumsiness that caused this whole unfortunate chain of events."

"I didn't do it on purpose, sir. It was an accident."

He narrowed his eyes. "Accident or not, you have caused a great deal of disruption. You will write Martin Champion a note, apologising for the trouble you caused. Now get out of my sight!"

After all the excitement in the morning, the rest of the day was a bit of an anti-climax. Nan collared us at lunchtime, demanding to know exactly what had gone on at the food demo. I managed somehow to persuade her that it was the sort of accident that could have happened to anyone, but she definitely wasn't happy. "Well," she sighed, "I hope you're telling the truth, because I had enough complaints about you two from Mr Bull last term to last me a lifetime, and I definitely don't want any more."

"That's an exaggeration," Donna grumbled as Nan marched off to supervise serving lunch. "It was only the one time we got in trouble." She was right, but although we were punished for taking part in the poker game with Jason Dundy, we could have got into even bigger trouble if Bull had found out how we'd been caught wandering around the Holtech offices without permission. I had got off lightly this time, but I needed to keep out of trouble from now on.

14

Death of a Kitchen Boy

By Thursday, everything was back to normal at Lea Green, although I got the impression that it wasn't just me who was trying to keep out of Mr Bull's way until the disastrous cookery demo had faded from his memory. Some of the teachers appeared to be doing the same, particularly Miss Leski.

It was raining at break-time, so instead of going into the yard, we met up with Jimmy and went off to the library to discuss what we'd found out from Sir John. We told him about how Furze had been given a glowing reference by an Arab prince, how Lady Coverly hadn't liked the atmosphere at the Priory, and how Parsons had a conviction for theft.

Jimmy, who wasn't looking his usual cheerful self, thanked us for our efforts, but we could tell his mind was somewhere else.

"What's up, Jimmy?" Donna asked. "Have more strange things been happening at the Priory?"

Jimmy shook his head. "No, but things are a bit difficult at home at the moment. Mum's upset because her ring's still missing, so whenever Dad goes out, she starts turning the place upside down trying to find it. Dad still suspects me of causing all the supernatural stuff, and I think something's worrying him too, because he's in a permanently bad mood. And Liddy's even grumpier than usual, because Furze still hasn't apologised for calling her a liar."

Donna tried to cheer him up. "Never mind, you've got the party to look forward to. Tell you what, why don't you ask your mum and dad if we can come to the barbecue, so you have some friends to keep you company. We could help you look for the ring, and do some more ghost-hunting too. If we can prove it's one of the staff faking all the supernatural stuff, you'll be in the clear."

"Thanks, Donna," Jimmy said, starting to look a bit happier.

As we followed him down the passage to our classroom, I whispered to Donna. "Exactly how are we going to achieve all this? I bet you haven't a clue."

I was right. She hadn't.

On Friday Donna and I were sitting in the dining hall finishing off our lunch, when we were joined by Jimmy. He looked excited as he sat down.

"When I was in the library last night," he told us, "I thought I'd have another look for books on the history of the Priory. I found this book called *English Country Houses and their Ghosts*, and it had a chapter on the Priory. Look!" He burrowed in his school bag and brought out a thick volume with pages that were going brown at the edges. As we bent over to have a closer look, he thumbed through it until he found the right page. We started reading.

The story concerned Major William Coverly, the man in the portrait that had fallen off the wall. It seemed that a valuable ring had gone missing from his wife's bedroom, and the Major got it into his head that it was a twelve-year-old kitchen boy called Seth Greenway who had stolen the ring. Seth kept protesting that he was innocent, but the Major threatened to beat the truth out of him. Terrified, Seth escaped from the Major's grasp and fled across the hall and through the open cellar door. Unfortunately, he lost his footing on the uneven stone steps and fell down the stairs, breaking his neck. The missing ring was later found under Mrs Coverly's bed, trapped between two floorboards.

Donna shuddered. "Major Coverly sounds like a brute! No wonder I didn't like the look of him."

Jimmy pointed to the next paragraph. "Look, this is the really interesting part *Ever since the death of Seth Greenway, inhabitants of the Priory have complained that from time to time the sound of a crying child can be heard coming from behind the cellar door, and objects move from place to place, seemingly without human intervention.*"

We were all silent for a moment, taking in the information.

"Right," I said. "If all the disturbances were caused by the spirit of the kitchen boy, then the most likely place to find evidence of his presence is the cellar. After all, that's where he died."

Just then we were joined by Emerald, who wanted

to know what the book was that we were all finding so fascinating, so we showed her the story of Seth Greenway.

After we had read the story for the second time, Donna said what we were all thinking. "Isn't it odd that we're reading this story about a missing ring just as another ring has gone missing? That's a very strange coincidence."

Emerald, who had been staring thoughtfully into the distance, suddenly shook her head. "Of course it's not a coincidence! Don't you see? It's because another ring has gone missing that the ghost of the kitchen boy is making all these odd things happen now!"

Jimmy began to look really agitated. He pointed to the book. "I only came across this book because it was on the floor when I went into the library. I'm the only person who ever looks at the books in the library, so how did it get there? I think the ghost put it there for me to find!"

"Maybe the ghost could help us find the missing ring!"

I was joking, but Donna took me seriously. "That's a great idea!"

"Oh yeah? And how are we going to contact this ghost? We can't just call him up on a mobile."

Donna pointed at Emerald. "We don't need a mobile. We've got Em. She's psychic."

Emerald began to protest, but Jimmy and Donna both started trying to persuade her to help. "You won't have to actually do anything," Donna said. "On *Ghost in Residence* they always take a 'sensitive' with them to create the right atmosphere. Jimmy, can you get Emerald an invitation to the barbecue?"

We were interrupted by the voice of the teacher on dinner duty, reminding us that the lunch break was over. We had been so wrapped up in our discussion that we had ignored the bell for end of lunch, and now we were the only ones left in the dining hall. Hastily, we made our way to our next class.

★

While I was waiting for Donna outside the gates after school, I was joined by Jason Dundy. Jason's dad runs the betting shop in the high street, and it was Jason who organised the poker game that got us into so much trouble with Bull the previous term.

Jason pointed to Alf who, as usual, was leaning against the Rolls, reading *The Sporting Life*. "See him? He spends loads of time in our shop, betting on the horses. Dad told me he lost a lot of money last month on a horse called Shining Star that turned out not to be such a star after all. I reckon he's lost his touch." He winked at me, before heading off down the road to the bus stop.

After he had gone, I stared thoughtfully at Alf. If he really had lost a lot of money, maybe a valuable antique ring would be too much of a temptation for a former thief to resist?

After supper that evening we received a text from Jimmy: ALL OK 4 TOMORROW. SEE YOU 2 AND EM AT THE BARBECUE.

We were all set for our next ghost hunt.

15

The Barbecue

The Devlins' anniversary barbecue was due to start at 5pm. By the time we three arrived at 5.30 there were already loads of large, flashy cars parked in the forecourt.

"I feel sorry for Jimmy's mum," Donna said. "All she wanted was a small private party for their close friends, but Mr Devlin seems to have invited lots of other people too."

It was the first time Emerald had seen the Priory, and as we walked through the archway into the old stable-yard and under another arch into the garden, she sighed. "Isn't it beautiful here? I wish we lived in the countryside instead of in the middle of town."

The garden was already full of groups of people chatting and sipping drinks out of tall glasses. A little way from the house, a cooking area had been set up, with a couple of large barbecue grills and a huge medieval-style spit on which a large bit of meat was roasting. Next to the spit stood Martin Champion, wearing the same chef's hat and white apron he had worn for the cookery demo. He was talking to Jimmy's mum and dad. I hoped fervently I would be able to keep out of his way, because although I had spent ages composing a letter to him apologising for the accident on Wednesday, I wasn't at all confident he had forgiven me.

We stood there for a few moments, scouring the groups of guests for some sign of Jimmy, when he suddenly popped up right next to us. "I thought you'd never come!" he said.

We chatted for a bit, and then I asked Jimmy, "Do you think the chef has told your mum and dad what happened in the cookery class?"

"I'm not sure. I overheard him tell Mum he'd had 'a minor accident' the other day and hurt his leg." I thought the chef's pride had probably been hurt more than his leg, but it was another reason to keep well out of his way.

Over by the barbecue, Jimmy's mum gave a nervous laugh in response to something the chef had said. Donna was staring at her too. "Your mum doesn't look as if she's enjoying the party much, Jimmy," she said.

Jimmy began to steer us away from the crowds of guests. "I know," he said, lowering his voice. "Most of the people here are Dad's friends, not hers, and before the party she had to tell Dad that the ring was missing. He was furious, and they had a big argument. She still thinks it's all her fault it's lost."

"Your poor mum!" Emerald said. "Why don't we have a look for it now, whilst everybody's outside? We shouldn't assume it's been stolen if there's a chance she really did just mislay it."

Donna agreed with her. "When something gets lost at home, Nan always says, 'It'll be just where you thought it was, but hidden underneath something else.'

It's worth a go, isn't it, so long as nobody catches us snooping?"

Jimmy shrugged. "OK, but I know she turned her bedroom upside-down when the ring first went missing, so it's definitely not there."

"Alright," I said. "Forget upstairs. We'll concentrate on the ground floor. We could try out the EMF meter in the dining room and living room at the same time, and keep an eye open for a chance to get into the cellar."

Jimmy glanced at the large table where Furze was busy mixing cocktails and Mrs Liddell was laying out plates of food. "Nobody has any reason to go indoors at the moment. You're right: it's the ideal opportunity. Come on."

We followed him as he led the way out of the garden and through the conservatory into the house. There was nobody in the living room when we went in, but I noticed the picture of Sir William Coverly had been put back on the wall, complete with new glass. Emerald went pale the minute she saw the picture. "That's him, isn't it? The man who caused the boy's death?"

"How did you know?" I asked. There were lots of old oil paintings in the sitting room, but she had picked the right one instantly.

She shook her head. "I just knew."

I stood in front of the picture and got out my mobile, but when I switched on the EMF app, the reading was normal. "Well, there's no ghostly activity here at the moment. Let's get on with searching the room."

We looked absolutely everywhere: underneath every piece of furniture, in case it had fallen on the floor; down the side of all the chairs and sofas; and behind curtains.

While the other three were on their hands and knees peering under furniture, I searched among the piles of books and magazines lying around on the many small tables. Next to Mr Devlin's favourite armchair I found a battered copy of *Foolproof Investing,* while on the coffee table next to the cookery books belonging to Jimmy's mum was *100 Ways to Boost Your Confidence*. Something white lying underneath the coffee table caught my eye, and I bent down and picked it up. It was an empty pill container, like the ones Nan keeps in our bathroom cupboard. The label on the side said: 'Susan Devlin. Promexinol.' I shoved it in my pocket to check out later.

Although we raised an awful lot of dust, there was no sign of the ring. We had no better luck in the dining room, or in the hall, where we rummaged unsuccessfully through a large bowl of odds and ends that stood on an old oak chest by the front door. Jimmy told us his mother never went near the games room, the study or the library. That only left the kitchen, but that was out of bounds for the present in case we ran into one of the staff.

Finally, we tried the cellar door, but it was firmly locked. "Furze will have the key with him, so he can fetch more wine when it's needed," Jimmy said. "We can't do anything more here at the moment. I vote we go and have some food now. We can carry on making plans whilst we're eating."

The smell of roasting meat had drifted into the house through the open windows, and I realised I was ravenous. "Come on, then. Let's go."

16

The Haunting

By the time we got back to the barbecue, loads more people had arrived, and there was a lot of noise and laughter. There was music playing in the background, and a few couples were dancing on the newly-cut lawn. By now I was famished, and all I had eyes for was the table laden with food. There was certainly a huge selection to choose from. All the dishes had labels written in old-fashioned lettering explaining what they were. Some, like 'venison cooked in wine', and 'goose stuffed with egg and pork' were foods I'd never eaten before, but there were also more familiar things like cheese tarts and pork pies.

"The puddings look scrummy!" Donna said, eyeing the elderflower cheesecake. "I can't wait to get stuck in."

Just then, Parsons arrived at the table, carrying a tray of food. He was dressed in a white shirt and black trousers, and looked very glum. "Why are you here, Alf?" Jimmy asked him.

Alf made a face. "I can think of better ways to spend a nice summer evening than serving food to your dad's guests, but the waiter didn't turn up, so I got roped in to take his place." He moved away to serve two guests with plates of strawberries and cream, and we started to help ourselves to food. Once we had loaded up our plates, Jimmy led us to a bench under a large oak tree, a long way from where all the guests were gathered. While we ate and drank, we discussed Mrs Devlin's missing ring.

"So if it was stolen, who's the most likely suspect?" Donna asked.

"I suppose it's Alf," Jimmy said. "After all, he was a thief in the past. But he said this was his ideal job. Why would he risk losing it by stealing something?"

I remembered what Jason had told me yesterday. "He might need the money. He's a regular customer in the Dundys' betting shop, and Jason says he lost a large amount on a horse recently. I bet Alf didn't tell you that, Jimmy." Jimmy shook his head. "Look, I know it looks bad for Alf, but I reckon Liddy has just as good a motive for stealing. We know her daughter is hard up and she wants to help her."

Donna frowned. "It's a pity we haven't got anything on Furze. I'd love it to be him. He gives me the shivers."

"At least he doesn't creep up on you like Mrs Liddell," I said. "She's so quiet, you never hear her coming. She's like a ghost herself."

Donna turned suddenly to Emerald, who hadn't said anything for ages. "You're very quiet, Em. What's the matter?"

Emerald blinked. She looked startled, as if she'd just woken from a trance. "I was thinking about that poor kitchen boy who died in the cellar. Ever since we went in the house, I haven't been able to get him out of my mind."

"You're sensing something, aren't you?" Donna asked her.

Emerald looked uneasy. "It's as if he's trying to get in touch with me. It's scary." She gave a little shiver.

I looked around at the crowds of people laughing and chattering in the distance, and the ruined chapel, bathed in a pink glow from the setting sun. Dance music was booming out of big speakers nearer the house, and the smell of meat roasting on the barbecue drifted towards us. It was the most unghostly scene you could imagine. I thought Em was letting her imagination run away with her, but I didn't say so, because I didn't want to hurt her feelings.

After a while Jimmy and Em went off to fetch some more drinks, and I remembered something I wanted to check. I got out my mobile and typed 'Promexinol' into a search engine.

Donna glanced over at me. "What are you doing?"

I showed her the pill container I'd found. It appeared the drug was a type of anti-depressant. "If she's taking lots of tablets, that could be why she's so forgetful, couldn't it?"

Donna nodded. "They don't seem to be working, do they? She always looks miserable." Then, as we saw Jimmy and Emerald approaching with a tray of drinks, Donna muttered, "Better not say anything to Jimmy. We don't want to upset him."

After we had finished our drinks, Donna suggested we go back to the house while everybody was still outdoors, and keep an eye open for a chance to get into the cellar. Nobody else could think of a better plan, so we walked back up the long sloping lawn towards the house. There were still plenty of people clustered around the barbecue and the food table, and a moment later, Mr Devlin pushed through the crowd, calling loudly for Furze. When the butler appeared, he told him to fetch some more champagne from the cellar. "Very good, sir," said Furze, walking off towards the kitchen.

Jimmy steered us around a group of people talking to his mother, and into the conservatory. "If Furze is really busy, there's a good chance he'll forget to lock the cellar door," he said in a low voice.

Once in the living room, we peered cautiously round the door that opened onto the hall. We could hear voices coming from behind the open cellar door. "You take that case there," I heard Furze say, "and I'll carry this one." After a moment, Alf emerged from the cellar, carrying a large crate full of bottles, followed by Furze, carrying a similar crate. "This thing weighs a ton!" grumbled Alf. Furze didn't look at all sympathetic. "Hurry up, and mind you don't drop the crate!" he said, as he followed Alf down the passage to the kitchen.

Jimmy hurried over to the cellar door, and tried the handle. He did a thumbs-up. "He left the door unlocked! I knew he would. Come on!" He pulled the door open, switched the light on, and disappeared down the steps. The rest of us followed close behind. I went last, and kicked the door stop into place before pulling the door almost shut behind us.

This time the chill hit me the minute I reached the bottom of the steps. I heard Emerald draw in her breath sharply as she felt it too. Her eyes widened, and she clutched Donna's arm. "He's here!"

Before anyone else had a chance to speak, things started happening. An old tin can that was lying on its side against the wall started rolling across the floor, as if it was being pushed by an invisible force. There was a big thud, as if someone had dropped something heavy on the stone floor. Then came the sound of a child crying. It was quite soft at first, but it seemed to get gradually louder, until the sound was echoing off the stone walls.

At first I was so startled, I couldn't move. After a moment, though, I remembered why we were there. I reached for my mobile and fumbled around, trying to turn on the EMF app. The reading appeared on the screen, then immediately disappeared as the phone went dead. Then, just like before, the light went out.

The room was now pitch black, and the sound of the child crying seemed to be coming from every direction. Suddenly Donna cried out, "Look! Over there!" and I saw a tiny ball of light hovering a few feet above the ground. As the ball of light started to move around the room, the crying began to grow fainter.

I was so mesmerised by the sight of the glowing ball that I lost all sense of time. How long was it there? A few seconds? A few minutes? Then, as suddenly as it had appeared, the ball of light vanished and the crying faded away completely.

In the sudden silence, I felt the darkness wrap itself around me like a dense blanket. The cold air seemed to penetrate every part of my body and I started to shiver uncontrollably. "Let's get out of here!" Jimmy said, but before any of us could make our way out of the cellar, the room was once more flooded with light. I turned round and looked upwards. Standing at the top of the stairs, staring down at us with his strange hooded eyes, was the butler.

17

Caught in the Act

For a moment nobody moved or spoke. Then Furze came slowly down the steps. "What are you doing down here, Master Jimmy?" he asked. "And what was all that noise?"

"We were ghost-hunting," Jimmy blurted out. "And it wasn't us making the noise. It was the ghost!"

Furze raised his brows and glanced round at the four of us. "Oh, ghost-hunting, is it now? Are you sure it wasn't you creating all the sound effects?"

Jimmy started to protest. He was getting quite agitated, and as Furze approached him, he took a step backwards and accidentally bumped into one of the wine racks. It swayed precariously, and a small crate that had been placed on top of the rack overbalanced and crashed to the floor. As we all stared, appalled, the crate splintered, the wine bottles broke, and a river of wine spewed out over the flagstones.

"Now look what you've done! Those bottles are priceless. Your dad'll skin you alive for this!" As Furze got angrier, he lost his posh accent and he no longer sounded like a butler. Then, just as I began to feel genuinely scared of him for the first time, he seemed to pull himself together and turn back into a butler again. "Right!" he said. "Upstairs, the lot of you. Now!"

After locking the cellar door securely behind us, he frogmarched us through the kitchen, across the courtyard and back out into the garden. I was feeling bad, because we were supposed to be helping Jimmy, and now it looked as if we'd got him into even more trouble. I was worried about Emerald, too. She looked shell-shocked after what had just happened.

Furze glanced round the groups of guests, trying to pick out Mr Devlin. Before he could locate him, there was a sudden commotion in one of the groups. Several women stepped quickly backwards, out of the way of a large man in a dinner jacket and spotted bow tie, who was lurching from side to side and shouting loudly, although he wasn't making much sense. Furze let go of Jimmy, muttering "Don't move!" to us, and hurried off towards the swaying man.

Alf beat him to it. "Now, now, sir! We don't want any trouble, do we? Maybe it's time you went home." He took the man firmly by the arm and pointed him in the direction of the courtyard. Furze joined him, and together the two of them guided the man away from the party and under the archway to the yard.

"That was lucky!" Jimmy said. "Come on, let's scram before Furze comes back!" He led us down a path towards the old oak tree where we had eaten our meal, taking care not to bump into partygoers on the way. He needn't have bothered: none of them paid any attention to us. By now dusk was falling, and although light from inside the house lit up the top end of the garden, the shrubbery was bathed in shadows and the ruined chapel at the lower end was just a dark blur. We had barely reached the seat under the tree when, in the distance, we heard a woman scream loudly. We stopped dead, and everything went quiet for a moment. Then somebody shouted "What's going on?" and people started talking again in excited voices.

As we stared at the ruined chapel, two dark shapes emerged from the back of the building and moved off down the garden towards the cliff path. It was impossible to see them clearly in the fading light, but they seemed to glide effortlessly over the rough ground.

As they disappeared behind some large bushes, we could see that, nearer the house, a group of people were gathering round a woman who sounded hysterical. She was screaming something about monks and ghosts, and some of the other guests were trying to calm her down.

Jimmy pointed in the direction taken by the two ghostly figures. "Come on, quickly, before they disappear!" He was already running towards the chapel, and we followed close behind. By the time we reached it, there was no sign of the two monks, although we carried on down the path from the chapel as far as the gate leading to the cliffs.

Jimmy sighed with frustration. "Lost them!"

"Well, that's what ghosts do," Donna pointed out. "They appear, and then they disappear."

I walked over to the gate and rattled the latch. To my surprise, it opened easily. Somebody had forgotten to lock up before the party, which meant strangers could have got into the grounds quite easily. But remembering what had happened earlier in the cellar, even I was beginning to believe the forms we had seen might be genuine ghosts.

As we started to walk back down the path towards the chapel, a figure appeared, walking briskly towards us. "Oh no! It's Dad!" Jimmy muttered. "Furze must have told him about the wine."

We stood still and waited for the storm to break. It was even worse than we had expected: not only had Furze told Jimmy's dad about the broken wine bottles, he had also accused us of playing at being ghosts. Now Mr Devlin was even more certain that it was Jimmy – with or without our help – who had caused all the supernatural phenomena. And our presence now on the far side of the chapel convinced him that we had somehow been responsible for the appearance of the two monks a few minutes earlier. Then he turned his attention to me. "And Martin tells me you caused a great deal of trouble at the cookery demonstration. Jimmy should choose his friends more carefully." He glared at Jimmy, who by now was looking very miserable indeed. "You're grounded, boy, for the foreseeable future, and your friends won't be welcome here either. I'm going to get Parsons to drive them home now, and as for you, you can go to your room and stay there!"

As Donna, Emerald and I followed Jimmy's dad back up to the house, nobody spoke. There was nothing left to say. Most of the remaining guests had gone indoors now, and the music had been turned off. Even Martin Champion had left. Whilst Jimmy disappeared into the house, and Mr Devlin tried to find Parsons, I was hoping desperately that he wouldn't complain about us to Nan.

18

The Poisoned Chalice

All through Sunday we were on edge, waiting for a phone call from Jimmy's dad complaining about our behaviour at the barbecue. When the phone finally rang, at about three o'clock in the afternoon, I braced myself for a tirade from Nan. I needn't have worried. The call was from Dad.

Since he left a week ago, we hadn't heard a word from him. That's typical of Dad: communication's never been his strong point. After Nan realised the call was from him, she put the phone on speaker so we could all hear what he had to say. "I'm surprised you're ringing now," she said. "Isn't it the middle of the night over there?"

Nan, like most adults, is obsessed with time. It's always school time, or meal time, or bedtime. It's never the right time to just hang out and enjoy yourself. Dad's different. Once he's working on an idea, it doesn't matter much to him what time it is, or even whether it's day or night. I could almost see him frowning and looking around for a clock. "It's nearly dawn, I think. I've been up all night following up a line of research. My head was buzzing with ideas, so I couldn't sleep." After explaining briefly where he had been and who he had met, he asked, "And how are Alex and Donna?"

Nan handed the phone to me, and I gave him a carefully edited account of the Devlins' barbecue, which didn't mention ghosts or poltergeists or monks. In fact, I made the whole thing sound rather dull. As I finished up with "And the medieval feast was great," Donna grabbed the phone off me and asked him when he was coming home.

"Next Sunday, if all goes well. In the meantime, be good. I don't want to hear any complaints about bad behaviour when I get back."

"You won't," Donna promised him, rather recklessly I thought, given recent events. "I'll be angelic, truly I will!" Behind her back, Nan raised her eyebrows.

I felt more cheerful after speaking to Dad, and we were both beginning to think that if Mr Devlin was going to ring Nan to complain about our behaviour, he would have done so earlier. We had tried ringing Jimmy, but he wasn't picking up. I guessed his dad had confiscated his phone as a further punishment. Donna had spoken to Emerald, who said that during the night she had had bad dreams involving the ghost boy. "I don't ever want to go back to the Priory," she said. "At least, not whilst his spirit is still hanging around there."

I still wasn't sure what to believe, but I was beginning to think Emerald might be right. Maybe all the weird things we had seen and heard over the weekend really did have a supernatural cause.

Jimmy's class went off on a school trip on Monday, so we didn't see him at all. In the afternoon, we had our art class with Miss Lovelace. It's Donna's favourite lesson, because she's really good at drawing. As usual, I sat at the back of the room with all the other kids who, like me, are rubbish at art, and hoped Miss Lovelace would forget to look at my work.

Miss Lovelace started to hand round a selection of pictures. "Today we are going to look at the art of the cartoonist, and examine some famous examples," she said, smiling gently at us through her thick glasses. "And after we have discussed some of the examples, I want you all to have a go at drawing your own cartoon."

Towards the end of the lesson, Ryan, Jason and I were looking at some 1950s comics that Miss Lovelace had brought in, and making half-hearted attempts to come up with our own superheroes. After a while I became aware of a lot of giggling going on at the table where Cat Williams was sitting with her mate Jasmin and some other cronies. I don't like Jasmin much, but even her worst enemy would have to admit that she's pretty good at drawing – almost as good as Donna, in fact. I wondered what she had drawn that was so funny. Eventually someone at the next table snatched the drawing off her and soon it was circulating round the class.

Miss Lovelace, who never pays much attention to what's going on behind her back, was busy talking to Donna and Emerald, who were sitting at the front. There was a lot of snickering as the drawing was passed round, and when it reached me I saw why.

For years Dad has had a reputation as the town eccentric. Because he doesn't care what other people think of him, he wears odd clothes, and often goes around muttering to himself. Other kids often tease us about him, and Donna's always found it much more difficult to ignore the taunts than I have. Today Cat and Jasmin had obviously decided that Dad would make a really good subject for a cartoon.

The picture showed a tall man with wild-looking hair, dressed in a strange assortment of clothes, who was obviously meant to be Dad. On one side of him were a boy and a girl in Lea Green uniforms, and on the other was a woman in an apron carrying a frying pan who was clearly Nan. They were all standing in front of a house with a big sign over the door saying 'Welcome to Loony Lodge.'

The class fell silent as everybody watched to see what my reaction would be. I could feel my face going red, but I didn't dare say anything, because I didn't want Donna to find out what had happened. Her temper is a lot worse than mine, and I didn't like to think what she would do if she saw the cartoon. In the end, since Donna had her back to me, I held the drawing up in the air where Jasmin could see it, crumpled it slowly into a ball, and put it in my pocket. Jasmin glared at me. She couldn't complain to Miss Lovelace that I'd destroyed her work, because Miss Lovelace would never have approved of such an unkind cartoon. This time I'd got the better of her, but I hoped fervently that Dad's robot would soon be on sale, and we would be free to tell everyone just how clever he really was.

★

That evening, after we had finished supper, Nan asked if we had any homework to do. I shook my head.

"Right, then. Why don't we all sit down and watch *The Poisoned Chalice*? I've just borrowed the DVD off one of the ladies I work with."

Donna, who had been unusually quiet at supper, was looking preoccupied, but she followed me and Nan into the sitting room and sat down obediently on the sofa while Nan set up the DVD. I wondered if she'd found out about the cartoon from somebody else. If she had, she clearly didn't want to talk about it.

The Vintage Films logo came up on the screen and then disappeared, replaced by a panoramic shot of the Priory and its grounds, and the date 1272. It was evening, and rain was pouring down as a party of riders came into view, accompanied by some horse-drawn carts loaded with baggage. They rode up to the Priory and knocked on the door. They were welcomed by the Prior, and we soon discovered that Lady Alys (played by the latest Hollywood sensation) was on her way to London to marry a man she had never met, and the travellers needed somewhere to stay for the night.

Although I was curious to see what parts of the house and grounds they had used in the film, I didn't expect to be interested in the story itself. Historical dramas aren't really my thing, but the story got a lot more interesting when Alys's sister Maud was found dead in her bed and the film turned into a murder mystery. I love murder mysteries, so from then on I started to pay more attention.

The huge, stone-flagged hall of the Priory became

the monks' dining hall. There were lots of monks in black robes, dining in the hall and worshipping in the chapel, but not many of them had speaking parts. I could see why they had needed lots of extras.

Since Alys refused to move on until her sister's murderer was caught and punished, the Prior appointed a young monk (played by another hot young Hollywood actor) to try to unmask the killer. Of course he and Alys fell in love, and after that it all got a bit too soppy for me. Eventually, after the killer (a fat monk with a squint) had finally been found and punished, Alys had to say a tearful goodbye to the young monk and continue her journey to London.

"Oh, I do love a good weepie!" Nan said, dabbing at her wet eyes with a tissue. "What did you think of it, Donna?"

Donna, who looked as if she had been miles away, jumped. "Oh, er… I think I prefer stories with happy endings." She yawned suddenly. "Nan, I'm really tired. I'm going to have an early night."

"Fine, lass," Nan said. "I'll see you in the morning."

After Donna had gone upstairs, Nan asked, "Is anything up with Donna, Alex? I've hardly heard a squeak out of her all evening."

I didn't know what to say. I wanted to tell Nan how Cat and Jasmin were picking on Donna, but I knew Donna would be angry with me if I mentioned it. I shrugged. "I expect she'll be OK tomorrow. I'm going up too, Nan. Got to get my things ready for the morning." The film had sparked an idea that I wanted to investigate, and I couldn't wait to check it out.

I switched on my laptop as soon as I got to my room. I was trying to remember what Jimmy had told us when we first arrived at the Priory about the monks who used to live there. Hadn't he said they were Franciscans?

I typed 'the Priory, Holcombe Bay' into the search engine. Immediately a page of results popped up. The longest entry was titled 'Historic Buildings on the South Coast' and gave a short history of several ancient houses and castles in our area, including the Priory. The article confirmed what I suspected: the monks who lived there had belonged to the Franciscan order. I also learned that while in more recent times Franciscans wore dark habits, the monks who lived in the medieval priory wore white habits, made out of unbleached sheep's wool.

That raised an interesting question: if all the shadowy figures seen gliding round the Priory and its grounds over the last two weeks really had been ghosts of the original Franciscan monks, why were they wearing black robes, rather than white ones?

19

The Gofer

The next morning Donna slipped out of the house early while I was still in my room, trying to find part of my PE kit that had gone missing. I guessed she was going to collect Emerald and walk to school with her. That confirmed my suspicion that she had found out somehow about the cartoon, and was upset about it. Whenever Donna's anxious about anything, she spends more time with Emerald, because Em is good at calming her down.

Donna went off with Em at break-time, giving me the chance to speak to Jimmy at last. There were some questions I needed to ask him, but when I started to talk, he cut me short. "Listen! Something really suspicious happened yesterday. Dad wanted to speak to Furze about something, and the intercom between the house and the staff flats wasn't working, so he asked me to go and find him. I went up the stairs beside the stable block to his flat. When I reached the front door, it was open slightly, and I could hear Furze talking to somebody on the phone. I thought I'd wait until he'd finished his call. Then I realised he sounded different from normal, and I started listening."

"Different? How?"

"He had a different accent, not his posh butler voice. He sounded more like Alf. He was giving someone instructions on how to get to the Priory. I heard him mention wine several times. I thought maybe he was arranging a delivery of some wine Dad had ordered, but then he said, 'It has to be Saturday. That's the only time they'll all be out.' He must have rung off after that, because he suddenly opened the front door. When he saw me, he glared at me and asked what I was doing there."

"What did you say?"

"I explained that Dad had sent me to find him, but I don't think he believed me. He said, 'Staff quarters are off limits to you, my lad.' I knew he was angry, because it's the first time he's ever forgotten to call me Master Jimmy. It was only afterwards I thought how suspicious it sounded, talking about doing something when everyone was out. Ever since then I've been wondering if he could be planning to steal Dad's wine collection."

"Do you think he realises you overheard him?"

Jimmy chewed his thumb. "I'm not sure. I know Sir John said Furze had impeccable references, but I don't trust him anymore."

"References can be faked. And anyway, I'm beginning to think he's not quite what he pretends to be. It's a pity we can't ask Harry what he thought of Furze."

"*Everything* would be better if only Harry was back home," Jimmy said. He looked thoroughly miserable. I told him there were a few leads I still had to follow up, and promised to let him know if I discovered anything useful.

After school Donna went home with Emerald. She told Nan she wouldn't be back until after supper, which meant I had a chance to carry out some private research. When I got home I cadged a drink and half a packet of biscuits off Nan and went upstairs to my room. The first thing I did was to find the telephone number of Vintage Films on their website. Taking a deep breath and crossing my fingers, I dialled the number for Vintage Films.

"Good afternoon, Vintage Films. How can I help you?" said a posh-sounding voice.

"Er… I'd like to speak to Harry Devlin."

"Certainly, sir. Who shall I say is calling?"

"Alex Macintyre."

"Just putting you through, sir."

For a moment I was bombarded with electronic music, then it died away and a voice came on the line. "This is Harry Devlin. What can I do for you?"

His voice was an older version of Jimmy's but more confident. Now I was finally speaking to him, I was tongue-tied. Eventually I mumbled, "I'm a friend of Jimmy's."

There was silence for a moment, then he said, "Is Jimmy with you?"

"No, I'm on my own. He doesn't know I'm calling you."

"So you guessed where I was, did you? I knew someone would eventually. How did you know?"

"It wasn't too difficult. Jimmy told me you'd been an extra in *The Poisoned Chalice* and that you fell out with your dad because he wouldn't let you become an actor.

Vintage Films seemed the logical place for you to start if you wanted a job."

He laughed. "Proper little sleuth, aren't you? Yeah, I'd made a few contacts during the filming, so the first thing I did when I left home was to follow them up and see what they could offer me. In the end I persuaded them to give me a job as a gofer."

"Gofer?"

"Odd-job man, basically. All the things nobody else wants to do. So how is everyone at the Priory?"

"Well… things are a bit difficult at the moment. You see, all these spooky things have been happening, and your dad believes it's just Jimmy playing tricks, so he's in big trouble. And your mum has lost a valuable ring, and Jimmy thinks Furze is up to no good…"

There was a short silence on the other end of the line, then Harry sighed. "I've been meaning to go home and try and make things up with Mum and Dad. I guess I can't put it off any longer. Maybe it's a good thing you found me when you did."

I sensed he was preparing to ring off, but there was still one thing I needed to know. "When they were filming at the house, was Furze friendly with any of the crew?"

"Not the crew, no, but I seem to remember he knew several of the cast. Sorry, Alex, but I have to go now. Work to do, you know?" The line went dead.

It didn't matter. I'd got what I wanted.

20

The Battle of the Somme

It was Wednesday afternoon, and Donna had been in a bad mood all day – spiky and unapproachable. Even Emerald was fed up with her. "She's just impossible at the moment!" she complained to me as we ate our lunch in the dining hall. "It's all Cat's fault. She and Jasmin are winding her up. I keep telling her to ignore them, but she won't listen to me." Em was right, of course. I don't bother telling Donna what to do anymore, because she just does the opposite. If I'd known what was going to happen next, I might have made the effort.

Our first lesson after lunch was science, and at 1.45pm groups of Year 8 kids started traipsing across the muddy area of grass nicknamed 'The Somme' on the way to the Science block. It was a blisteringly hot day, and Charlie Carter, the caretaker, was using a hose to water some drooping flowers in the one remaining flower bed. Cat and Jasmin were walking side by side in the first group, while Donna was following further behind. I saw Jasmin lean over and whisper something to Cat. She giggled, then she turned round and glanced at Donna before whispering something back to Jasmin. You could tell they were talking about Donna.

Donna glared back. “Don’t you dare say nasty things about my dad, Cat Williams!”

Cat turned round and faced Donna. She was smirking. “Why shouldn’t I? You know they’re true!”

“You’re a filthy liar!” Donna shouted and suddenly, out of the blue, she launched herself at Cat, who squealed as she fell backwards onto the grass. Jasmin jumped sideways out of the way as the two of them rolled over. Cat, still squealing, was desperately trying to get away from Donna, but Donna had a firm hold on her and wouldn’t let go.

By now there was a ring of kids around the two struggling figures, and people were starting to take sides and shout encouragement. As Donna and Cat rolled around on the ground, the noise level rose, and more and more kids started to come outside to see what was going on.

When Cat got a firm grip on Donna’s hair and pulled hard, Donna tried to get Cat’s arm away from her head, but all she managed to do was grab the sleeve of Cat’s blouse, which ripped at the seam. I was vaguely aware that Em was standing beside me shouting “Go for it, Donna!” I just stood there, unable to decide what to do. I was Donna’s big brother (even if I was only ten minutes older than her) and it was my job to look out for her, but I didn’t fancy my chances of escaping unhurt if I tried to stop the fight.

As I dithered, I noticed Charlie Carter edging closer to the two writhing figures. He was still holding the hose, which was gushing water onto the ground. Suddenly, without warning, water came shooting out of the hose in a perfect arc and descended on Donna and Cat. They both squealed and rolled away from each other as Charlie pointed the hose back down towards the ground. Everyone went quiet as Charlie scratched his head. "Oops, sorry, girls," he said. "Didn't mean to do that. Blooming thing just slipped out of my hand." But he didn't look at all sorry.

Cat staggered to her feet and tried to shake the water off her clothes. "She tore my blouse!" she wailed, glaring at Donna, who was still sitting down, looking as if she was about to cry. It was just at that moment that Mr Bull arrived on the scene, closely followed by Miss Wren. The veins on Bull's forehead were throbbing, and his bald head was turning pink, which is always a bad sign. "What the devil is going on here?" he shouted. Then he spotted Donna. "Donna Macintyre! I might have guessed! Wherever there's trouble, there's always a Macintyre around! And why, may I ask, are you both dripping wet?"

I looked around for the caretaker but he had slipped away, taking the hose with him. Mr Bull stared at Cat. "Well?"

Cat pointed at Donna. "It's all her fault, sir! She attacked me."

Mr Bull strode over to where Donna was sitting. "On your feet!" he snapped, glaring down at her. He was breathing hard, and his face was contorted with anger so that he looked like one of those scary gargoyles you see on old churches. As Donna got shakily to her feet, Mr Bull looked from her to Cat. "Both of you to my office now!" he roared. "And the rest of you – get to your lessons!"

As Bull escorted the two of them back into the main building, Miss Wren caught sight of me and came over to where I was standing. Because she's Dad's girlfriend, she knows us quite well, and I hoped she might stand up for Donna.

"Who started the fight, Alex?" she asked.

There didn't seem any point in lying about it; too many other people had seen what happened. "Donna did," I said. "But Cat and Jasmin have been baiting her for days. She just couldn't take it anymore."

Miss Wren sighed. "I'll do what I can for her," she said, but she didn't sound very optimistic. She disappeared back into the main building, and I turned and headed off to the Science block.

21

Up to No Good

Donna never turned up for the science lesson, and I was desperate to find out what had gone on in Mr Bull's study. When the lesson finished, I was just about to try and find Miss Wren when I saw her waiting outside the classroom door.

As the other kids streamed out into the corridor, she drew me aside. "I did speak up for Donna, but Mr Bull overruled me. Donna and Cat have both been suspended for the rest of the week. I had a free period, so I drove Donna home. I explained to your Nan that it wasn't entirely Donna's fault, but she wasn't best pleased, as you can imagine."

I thanked Miss Wren for trying to help Donna, before dashing off to find Jimmy. Now that he was grounded and without a phone, I needed to catch him before he went home. Luckily I bumped into him in the yard before he got as far as the waiting Rolls.

"We need to talk. Get Alf to tell your mum you've got an after-school club, and arrange for him to pick you up in an hour's time."

Jimmy grinned. "Alf will be pleased. It'll give him a chance to place a few bets!" He disappeared, then returned a few minutes later, doing a thumbs-up. We hung around in the yard until the Rolls had driven off, then we crossed the road to the piece of scruffy waste land opposite the school where a few bored-looking kids were kicking a ball around. We sat down on a bench covered in ancient bird droppings, and I told Jimmy that I had found his brother.

Jimmy was so pleased, I thought he was going to hug me. He calmed down after a bit, and I told him how I'd worked out where Harry was. "I think he wants to patch things up with your mum and dad, so he'll probably be home soon. But that's not the only thing I've found out…" I explained how we had watched *The Poisoned Chalice*, and how the costume department had got the colour of the monks' robes wrong.

Jimmy looked puzzled. "Why is that important?"

"Because while the monks who lived at the Priory originally wore white robes, the ghostly monks everyone has been seeing lately all wear black robes. If they were the real spirits of dead monks, they'd be wearing white robes, wouldn't they?" Before Jimmy could reply, I continued. "And there's something else. About Furze. Sir John told us that he had spoken to some Arab prince, who claimed to be Furze's previous employer and said all sorts of nice things about him. But maybe he wasn't really an Arab prince at all. Maybe he was an actor putting on a foreign accent." Jimmy looked dubious as I went on. "Harry said Furze was friendly with some of the cast of *The Poisoned Chalice*, and Donna said after she first met him that he was 'just like a butler in a film.' I think he's an actor who's just pretending to be a butler."

Jimmy stared at me. "Why…?" he began, then he stopped. "Of course! There are lots of valuable things at the Priory, aren't there? Dad's wine collection, Mum's ring…"

I nodded. "The ring's already disappeared. If he believes you overheard that conversation he was having, he'll know he hasn't got much time."

Jimmy shook his head. "How can we stop him? We haven't got any proof he's planning anything. It's all just a theory."

"Can't you tell your mum or dad what you suspect?"

Jimmy sighed. "The last few days, Dad has spent most of his time locked in his study. I don't know what's going on, but he seems to be really worried about something. Whenever I try and talk to him, he says, 'Not now, son.' And Mum's not much better. It's as if she's in a dream world the whole time."

That was when I remembered the pill bottle I'd found, belonging to Mrs Devlin. "Did you know your mum is taking anti-depressants? If she's taking a lot of them, that could be why she seems to be miles away most of the time."

The minute I'd said it, I wished I'd kept my mouth shut, but it was too late. Jimmy glared at me. "Are you accusing my mum of being a drug addict?"

"Of course not! It's only… well, you said she kept forgetting things. Maybe that's why she can't remember where she put the ring." I floundered to a halt as Jimmy got up off the bench, looking angry and upset.

"I'm going to find Alf," he said. "And in future, leave my mum out of it!"

I continued to sit on the bench for a few minutes after Jimmy had gone, kicking myself for having upset him. After seeing how Donna had reacted when Cat criticised Dad, I should have known better.

When I let myself in through the front door half an hour later, the house was ominously quiet. There were no sounds of Nan singing along to the radio, or pottering about in the kitchen as she usually did. I poked my head around the sitting room door, and saw her slumped in an armchair with her eyes closed. It was so unlike her that for a moment I panicked.

"Nan?"

I needn't have worried. Her eyes flew open and, before I was even through the door, she had launched into a tirade about Donna and her bad behaviour. It seemed to go on and on, and just when I thought she had finished, she started on me. "And it's only a week since *you* caused all that trouble at the cookery demo…"

I was getting heated now too. "That's not fair! It wasn't me who burned the lemon curd and forgot to switch off the oven."

I might as well not have bothered. Nan ignored me and continued sounding off until eventually she ran out of steam. She shook her head and sighed heavily. "When Donna promised your dad she was going to be good, I knew it was tempting fate. Why is Ian never here when he's needed?" With another sigh, she got up and went out of the room.

I left her to it and went upstairs to Donna's room. I found her lying on her bed, staring at the ceiling. She had wet cheeks and puffy eyes, and I guessed she had been crying.

When she saw me, she looked up. "I refused to apologise to Cat for having a go at her. She deserved it. That made Bull even angrier."

I sat down on the bed. "Are you going to tell me what it was all about?"

"She's been making digs at me all week. You know: my hair's a mess, my clothes are out of date, I should use more deodorant – the usual stuff. Then somebody told me about that horrible cartoon." She glared at me. "Why didn't *you* tell me about it?" Before I could answer, she carried on. "Then today she started on Dad. It was when she called him a weirdo that I finally flipped." She sniffed, and gulped back some tears. "If only we could tell people about the robot, then they'd realise how clever he is, but we promised not to!" She sniffed again.

She looked as if she was going to start crying again, so I tried to distract her. "Forget about Cat for a bit. I've got loads of stuff to tell you. For a start, I've found Harry Devlin."

That caught her attention. I explained how he'd got himself a job with Vintage Films and how, after watching *The Poisoned Chalice*, I'd realised that the figures in black robes were unlikely to be real ghosts. Then I told her about the phone call Jimmy had overheard, and my theory that Furze was really an actor. "Harry said Furze knew several of the actors in the film. He could have got one of his actor friends to put on a foreign accent and pretend to be an Arab prince to give him a reference. If he's not a real butler, and he's planning to steal stuff from the Priory, he'll want to get a move on if he thinks Jimmy overheard his phone conversation. If we want to stop him, we have to do something fast."

"Why doesn't Jimmy just tell his parents what he suspects?"

I explained what Jimmy had told me about the situation at the Priory. "They already think he's a troublemaker, and neither of them seems to be in any mood to listen to him. If we could get some proof that Furze is up to no good, then they'd have to listen."

"There's no time left to get proof, if he's planning something for this weekend. We need to try and stop him."

"So how do we do that?"

That was the billion-dollar question.

22

A Phone Call from a Ghost

As I walked past the entrance to the Lea Green estate on the way to school the next morning, I was joined by Emerald. She knew about Donna's suspension because Donna had phoned her the night before. Donna was lucky that Nan hadn't confiscated her phone, although she had stopped her pocket money for a month.

"Was your nan very angry with her?"

I nodded. "Nan had a go at me too when I got home. She's going to go into meltdown if either of us gets into any more trouble this term."

"Poor Donna!" Emerald said. Then, unexpectedly, she changed the subject. "After all those weird things happened in the cellar on the day of the barbecue, do you still think there's no such thing as ghosts?"

I hesitated. Despite the evidence about the colour of the monks' robes, I was still unsure what I believed. "Why do you ask?"

She was silent for a moment, then, "Ever since the barbecue, I've been having these strange dreams. I'm on my mobile, and the person I'm talking to wants to tell me something important, but every time he's just about to tell me what it is, the phone dies. I wake up feeling really frustrated."

"So who is this person you're talking to?"

"That's the really weird bit. I think it's that kitchen boy, the one who fell down the cellar stairs." She glanced sideways at me, and then looked quickly away again. "Do you think I'm being silly?"

I didn't know how to reply, because I couldn't say 'yes' without offending her. "I might believe it really is the ghost boy," I said eventually, "if he actually tells you something only he would know."

She made a face. "Well, I wish he'd hurry up and tell me, because it's scary getting a phone call from a ghost, even if it is only in a dream."

All morning I'd been feeling guilty about falling out with Jimmy, so after lunch I went looking for him. I found him sitting on his own in the library, staring into space. I started to mumble an apology for upsetting him the day before, but he cut me short. "Never mind that. Do you think Alf could be involved in whatever Furze is planning?"

"What makes you say that?"

"He's about the only person left at the Priory that I can still talk to, and he's normally really chatty, but on the drive to school today, he looked quite grim. He obviously had something on his mind, so I asked him what the matter was. 'Nothing to concern you, Jimbo,' he said, and started talking about something else." Jimmy sighed. "I don't want him to be the thief, but if he's lost a lot of money, he might be tempted to steal something, mightn't he?"

It was worrying that we might have two thieves to deal with instead of just one. "Perhaps it'd be safer for the moment to just assume we can't trust Alf," I suggested. Then I remembered there was something I needed to find out from Jimmy. "Furze said you were all going to be out on Saturday. What's going on?"

"It's my great-aunt's eightieth birthday, and we're taking her out for lunch. Afterwards Dad has promised to drive her to some famous beauty spot along the coast. Mum has given all the staff the day off."

Only two more days to go, I thought. We didn't have much time left, and we still didn't have a plan. I tried to reassure Jimmy that we were working on a scheme for foiling any robbery that might take place. I didn't let on that we still didn't have a clue how to do that.

★

When I got home, Donna was waiting for me. "Listen, I've thought about what we were discussing the other night. If Jimmy's afraid there's going to be a robbery, and his mum and dad won't listen to him, then the obvious people to tell are the police. After all, it's their job to prevent crime, isn't it, so they'd *have* to listen to us."

She was right, of course, but I hesitated. A few years ago I'd gone to the police station with Nan after my bike was stolen, and I still remembered how the huge sergeant who took our details had scared the life out of me. I was older and bigger now, but I still didn't fancy the idea. I can never hide my feelings from Donna, though, and she picked up on my hesitation instantly.

"You're scared, aren't you? If you won't go, I'll go on my own."

That settled it. "Don't be silly. Of course I'm not scared. We'll go tomorrow, after school. We can tell Nan we're going round to Emerald's."

★

When I got back from school on Friday afternoon and walked into the kitchen, Donna and Nan were in the middle of an argument.

"But I *promised* Emerald we'd go round this evening!"

"Well, she'll have to do without you for once. I'm not having you gallivanting around enjoying yourself when you're on suspension. Your social life is on hold until you're back at school."

Donna opened her mouth to answer back, but I shot her a look and butted in. "Don't worry, Donna. I'll go round to Emerald's and give her back that DVD you borrowed. That'll be alright, won't it, Nan?"

Nan looked suspiciously at us both, but after a moment she nodded. "Fine, Alex. Just make sure you're back in time for supper."

★

That was how, later that afternoon, I found myself getting off the bus in the centre of town, before crossing Market Square and making my way down the side street that led to the police station. Without Donna for moral support, I was nervous as I stepped over the threshold and walked up to the counter, although I did my best to hide it. This time the sergeant facing me was a woman. She looked me up and down as I approached, a bit like a farmer assessing a cow on sale in the local cattle market.

"Yes?" she said, and she didn't sound friendly.

For a moment I couldn't get any words out. I cleared my throat. "Umm… I want to report something suspicious."

The sergeant, who had the sort of powerful shoulders you usually only see on a wrestler, leaned her elbows on the counter and stared at me. "Go on," she said. "I'm all ears."

I could feel my cheeks starting to go pink with anger. I don't like being patronised, but I couldn't afford to show it. "There's a man called Ebenezer Furze who works as a butler at the Priory, the old house just outside town where my friend Jimmy lives. I don't think he's a butler at all. I think he got the job by giving false references, and now he's planning some sort of robbery."

The sergeant raised her eyebrows. "Got any evidence of this?"

I was getting fed up with her staring at me as if I was a prize bull. "Not yet, but an antique ring has gone missing, and Mr Devlin has a valuable collection of vintage wines, and Furze has been making suspicious phone calls, talking to someone about wine. I think he has something planned for Saturday."

She sighed. "How old are you, sonny?"

Now, one thing that really annoys me is being called 'sonny.' I glared at her. "What's that got to do with anything?"

"Age?" she repeated.

"I'm thirteen," I snapped. "Not that it's any of your business. Look, can't you check him out on your database?"

Just then the outside doors flew open as two burly constables hauled a young man inside and dragged him, kicking and protesting up to the counter. "Drunk and disorderly," said one of the PCs, grinning at the sergeant. "He's all yours, Sarge."

The next moment, the young man threw up all over the counter. After that it was obvious the sergeant no longer had any time for me so, as she took custody of the young man, I escaped unnoticed through the automatic doors and out into the street.

As I began walking back towards the bus stop, I decided that was the last time I would try and be a responsible citizen. The sergeant plainly hadn't believed a word I said. It seemed that we were Jimmy's only hope now.

23

To Catch a Thief

Whilst Nan was cooking supper that evening, Donna and I brainstormed some ideas to try and prevent Furze carrying out his plans. It didn't help that we had no idea what those plans were, who his accomplices were, or exactly what time on Saturday everything was going to kick off. There was also the chance that Jimmy had misunderstood what he'd overheard, and Furze wasn't a criminal at all.

After a lot of arguing, we finally worked out a plan that seemed to make sense. However, we still weren't sure that Nan would let Donna leave the house, even though her suspension officially ended on Friday evening. If she was allowed out, we'd then have to concoct a story to explain where we were going and why we'd be out for such a long time. In the end Nan solved that problem for us by telling us over supper that she had been offered a four-hour cleaning job on Saturday in one of the big houses on Castleview. She would be going out at about 11.30 and wouldn't be back until late afternoon.

"You'll be alright on your own for a few hours, won't you? I'll leave some food out for your lunch." Then, as an afterthought, she added, "And if I come home and find either of you have got into any more trouble while I'm out, there will be SERIOUS consequences. Do I make myself clear?"

"Yes, Nan," we both said, but my heart sank. The stakes had suddenly got a lot higher, and there were no guarantees our plan would work.

According to Jimmy, his parents had arranged to pick up the great-aunt at midday on Saturday to take her to the restaurant, so he reckoned they would be leaving the Priory at about 11.30 – the same time Nan was due to leave for her cleaning job. As soon as she had disappeared down the street, we got our bikes out of the shed, and by 11.45 we were cycling as fast as we could towards the caravan park by the beach. This was where the path started that wound its way along the cliffs and past the back entrance to the Priory.

I'd managed to grab a few minutes with Jimmy at school the day before to explain the plan to him. "When your parents go out, Jimmy, you're going to have to pretend you're ill or something, so they leave you behind. Then make sure that gate onto the cliff path is unlocked, and we'll come up to the house through the shrubbery. We'll be less visible that way."

Jimmy nodded. "OK, but what are you going to do when you reach the house?"

"We'll have to play it by ear. If Furze is out, we'll start by having a look round his flat and see if we can find anything incriminating."

Jimmy looked doubtful. "The flat will be locked, won't it?"

"Maybe there's a spare key to the flat on that bunch of keys in your dad's study. See what you can find."

Jimmy agreed to do as I suggested, but we wouldn't know if he had managed to fool his parents until we arrived at the door in the wall. Half of me hoped that we would find it locked, and Jimmy nowhere to be seen. There were so many things that could go wrong with what we were planning. Even if Furze wasn't guilty of plotting a robbery, if he caught us searching his flat, the least he would do was report us to Mr Devlin. Jimmy would be in even worse trouble than he already was, and what Nan would say if she heard what we had been doing didn't bear thinking about.

It was another hot day, and by the time we reached the caravan park I was sweating heavily. There was a flight of steps from the caravan park up to the cliff path, so we left our bikes padlocked to some railings at the foot of the steps and continued on foot. By the time we reached the door in the wall, it was 12.10. By now, if everything had gone as planned, Jimmy's mum and dad should be well on their way to the restaurant with his great-aunt.

As I'd agreed with Jimmy, I knocked twice on the door. A moment later we heard the key jingling in the lock, and the door opened to reveal Jimmy, dressed in a pair of bright red pyjamas that clashed spectacularly with his ginger hair.

Donna did a double-take. "I know you're supposed to be ill, Jimmy, but isn't this taking things a bit far?"

Jimmy grimaced. "I told Mum I had a tummy upset and it wasn't safe for me to leave the house, but I was a bit too convincing. She didn't want to leave me on my own, and she was fussing so much I thought they'd never go. In the end Dad persuaded her I'd be fine for a few hours and they left, but I didn't have time to change before I came to meet you."

"Never mind that!" I said. "We need to hurry. We may not have much time. Are any of the staff still around?"

Jimmy shook his head. "Liddy left the house as soon as she had cleared away breakfast, and Alf and Furze went out soon afterwards. I haven't seen anybody return."

Although it sounded as if there was nobody to see us, we decided to approach the house by skirting the ruined chapel and going through the shrubbery so that we would be as inconspicuous as possible. Before we crossed the lawn, where there was no cover, we paused for a few minutes, watching and listening, but everything was still. The only sound was some wood pigeons cooing in the trees behind us.

"Come on!" Donna said. "Let's go!" We emerged from behind the bushes and ran quickly towards the old stable yard. Our trainers made no sound on the stone slabs that paved the yard as we hurried round the side of the building and up the stairs leading to the staff flats. At the top of the stairs was a little landing with two doors opening off it. Jimmy, who had managed to get the key ring from his dad's study, chose a key from the bunch and quickly opened the door on the left. "This is Furze's flat," he whispered. "The other one belongs to Alf."

Inside it was cool after the heat of the garden. The

first thing I noticed was that there were no pictures on the walls, no framed photographs, nothing that might give a clue as to what kind of man lived there.

"Come on, then. Where do we start?" Donna asked.

"He'll probably have his phone with him, but look for a laptop, a diary, papers... anything that might contain useful information. And keep your eyes open for the antique ring."

We started by searching the sitting room. The first thing we found, in a drawer in the desk, was a laptop. When I opened it up, though, we soon discovered that in order to read any of the files on it, we needed a password.

"Any budding computer hackers here?" I joked. But none of us had a clue how to find a way in without the password, and we couldn't spare time trying to figure out what that was, so we soon gave up on the computer.

"I'll check out the other rooms," Donna said, disappearing into the bedroom. She was back in a moment, looking excited. "He's cleared out his wardrobe, and there are two big suitcases full of clothes on the bed. Come and see!"

Jimmy and I followed her back into the bedroom. As well as the suitcases, there was a smaller bag like the one Dad had taken with him to America to hold his travel documents. Inside was a passport, a wallet containing some foreign money, and a thick paperback entitled *Great Wine Vintages of the Twentieth Century.* Furze had been doing his homework.

"Has he given in his notice?" I asked Jimmy.

Jimmy shook his head. "I don't think so. I'm sure I would have heard if he had."

"Then we were right. He's going to steal the vintage wine and do a runner before your mum and dad get back."

Jimmy bit his lip. "How can we stop him?"

I quickly explained the second part of the plan. The night before, when we were trying to come up with a way of stopping Furze stealing the wine, a picture had floated into my mind of Furze and Alf carrying crates of champagne out of the cellar on the night of the barbecue, while we watched from behind the living room door. "There's a lot of wine in that cellar. It's going to take several trips to get it all up the stairs, out of the house, and loaded into some sort of vehicle. If we hide somewhere near the cellar door, all we have to do is shut the door and lock it whilst he's down there. Then we can call the police."

Donna frowned. "But that doesn't prove he was going to steal the wine. He could make some excuse for being in the cellar."

"Not if we wait until he's already removed half the wine. Then it will be obvious what he's doing."

Jimmy was staring at the bunch of keys in his hand. "Hang on a minute. Furze will need a key to get into the cellar, and I've got Dad's keys here."

"He probably got the cellar key copied," Donna suggested. "Just in case he couldn't get hold of your dad's keys."

I glanced at my watch and realised, to my horror, that we had already been in the flat for half an hour. "We need to hurry up and get in place, because he and the friend with the van are bound to be here soon. Time's running out."

I'd barely finished speaking when we heard the sound of a vehicle rumbling into the courtyard below us. We'd left it too late, and now we were trapped in the flat.

24

The Golden Ball

As the vehicle drew to a halt in the yard, we all hurriedly moved back from the window so we were hidden from sight. Then Donna got down on her hands and knees and crawled back to the window, where she raised her head just high enough to see over the sill.

"What's going on?" Jimmy whispered.

"There's a large white van parked outside the back entrance. I can see two people in the front – one's Furze – and he's got someone else with him." She ducked her head down and turned to me. She looked panic-stricken. "What if they come up to the flat and find us?"

I prayed it wouldn't come to that. The wardrobe was about the only place we could hide, and that wasn't big enough for all three of us to fit inside. "Keep looking!" I whispered. "Then at least we'll get some warning if they're coming up here. Can you see the other man clearly? Is it Alf?"

Donna peered out again. "They're just getting out of the cab… I can't quite see… Oh, now I can. It's not Alf – he's short and fat and balding. Now Furze is going into the house, and the other man is opening up the back of the van. Oh, thank goodness, he's going into the house too!"

"He must be going to load up the wine before he comes back here for his stuff," Jimmy suggested. "We should get out of the flat now, whilst they're in the cellar. We can go round the back of the house and get in through the conservatory."

So, keeping our eyes and ears open for any sign of the two men returning, we left the flat, hurried down the stairs and slipped out under the arch into the garden. From there we ran along the side of the house until we reached the conservatory, which Jimmy unlocked using his bunch of keys. While Donna and I hid among the miniature forest of potted plants, Jimmy went ahead to check if the coast was clear. He was back before long, beckoning us to follow him into the living room. "They're in the cellar!" he hissed. "The door to the hall is slightly open, so we can hear them come and go while we hide in here."

We settled ourselves behind one of the huge sofas in the living room, where we could hear clearly if anyone came into the hall, but they couldn't see us if they poked their head around the door.

Very soon we heard feet ascending the cellar stairs, and then footsteps crossing the hall in the direction of the kitchen. The footsteps were slow and careful, as if the person was carrying something heavy. I guessed they were taking crates of wine out to the van in the yard.

"We need to wait until they're both back in the cellar before we lock the door," Jimmy whispered. "I'll go and peer round the door so we know when it's the right time." I nodded. I was sweating heavily and tense with anticipation, but so far everything seemed to be going according to plan. Only a few more minutes and Furze would be safely under lock and key.

More footsteps clattered across the hall and down the steps to the cellar. Jimmy turned and mouthed "Now?"

I shook my head. "Wait a bit longer." The more wine Furze had removed from the house, the more guilty he would look, and by my reckoning, there must be several crate-loads of wine still to go.

The footsteps returned, and then died away again as they descended to the cellar. I gave Jimmy a thumbs-up. I saw him poke his head round the door to make sure there was nobody in the hall, then he slipped out of the room. A few moments later he returned, with a wide grin on his face, holding up the bunch of keys. "Done it!"

"Well done, Jimmy!" Donna said. "Now we can phone the police, and this time they'll have to believe us!" As we got up from behind the sofa and walked over to join Jimmy, she was already getting out her mobile, but we were barely halfway across the room when suddenly the sitting room door swung open and a tall figure appeared in the doorway. It was Furze.

"I don't think that's a very good idea, Master Jimmy," he said.

Donna gave a little yelp and dropped the phone. We stared at each other, horrified. I just had time to wonder why Jimmy hadn't realised that only one man had gone back into the cellar before Furze put a hand into his pocket and withdrew a small, gleaming handgun.

"Don't anybody move," he said. He didn't sound threatening, but he didn't need to. The gun said it all for him. Continuing to point the gun at us, he quickly knelt down and picked up Donna's mobile. "Right," he said, as he straightened up. "Put your hands above your head and keep them there. I'm going to check your pockets. And don't try any stupid stunts. We don't want any accidents, do we?"

As we raised our arms, he delved into our pockets, removing my phone and Jimmy's bunch of keys, and establishing that Donna had nothing else of interest to him.

Suddenly we heard banging from behind the cellar door, and a muffled voice shouting something. As the shouting continued, Furze motioned us towards the door. "You're coming down to the cellar where I can keep an eye on you. Don't try anything, because I'm right behind you."

As we stumbled across the hall towards the cellar door, all I could think of was that somewhere behind me a gun was pointing at my back. Jimmy was shivering beside me, and Donna glanced sideways at me out of terrified eyes. When we reached the door, Furze gave the bunch of keys back to Jimmy and told him to unlock it, while he kept us covered with the gun. As the door opened, the other man appeared in the doorway. He was much shorter and fatter than Furze, and he had a squint in one eye. I recognised him immediately. He had played the murderous monk in *The Poisoned Chalice.*

When he saw us, his face darkened. "What the…?" he began, but Furze cut him short.

"We're late already," he said. "We'll get them down to the cellar and tie them up, then we'll clear the rest of the wine. We must be out of here before the parents get back."

The fat man threw us a really evil look before turning and going down the steps to the cellar. We followed him in single file, until we were standing together at the bottom of the stairs. Furze stood nearby, keeping the gun trained on us. "Have a look for something to tie them up with," he told his mate. "And hurry up! We don't have much time."

After scrabbling around for a bit, Furze's mate dug out a coil of thick garden twine from behind the wine racks and motioned to us to sit down with our backs to one of the huge stone pillars that supported the vaulted ceiling. While Furze continued to point the gun at us, the fat guy swiftly tied Jimmy's hands together behind his back and then bound his feet together.

He'd finished tying Jimmy up and had just started on Donna when I was gripped by the familiar chill we had felt twice before. Then the noise began. This time, though, it didn't sound like a child crying. This time it sounded like the murmuring of many voices.

The fat man gave a start and turned to Furze. "What's going on, mate?"

Furze cast a furious glance at us. "It must be those wretched kids again. I don't know how they're doing it, but for weeks now they've been pretending to be ghosts, fiddling with the lights and making strange noises. Just ignore them."

The fat man still looked uneasy, but he went back to tying Donna's hands and ankles, pulling the twine so tight that she winced. He was just about to start on me when the light suddenly flickered and died. The instant the light went out, the murmuring voices also stopped abruptly. Suddenly the room was pitch black and completely silent. The temperature still felt arctic, and I was shivering uncontrollably.

Although I couldn't see anything, I sensed the fat man getting up and moving away from us, and I could hear him blundering around and knocking into things. Then Furze's voice startled me, coming out of the darkness. "Stay where you are, you fool. I don't want you knocking over one of those crates of wine!"

The next moment, the fat man let out an oath. "Look! Over there!"

I couldn't understand how he could see anything in the blackness, but as I turned my head towards the nearest wall, I noticed a glowing ball of light, just like the one we had seen last time we were in the cellar. This time, though, it wasn't just flitting from place to place; it was moving slowly along the wall from left to right, following some sort of pattern. As I watched, mesmerised, I realised it was spelling out a word on the wall. Donna was following it too, muttering the letters under her breath. "T… H… I… E… F… Thief!"

The golden ball vanished as soon as the word was completed, but the letters remained, as though sprayed onto the wall with fluorescent paint. They were like bright candles, lighting up the darkness.

"That's no kid's trick!" the fat man said in a shaking voice. "Come on, mate, let's get out of here!"

"Not without the rest of the wine!" Furze said. "There are only six more crates left. I'm not giving up now!" In the dim glow from the illuminated letters, I saw him pick up a crate and move towards the stairs. His friend cast one more glance towards the letters on the wall, then picked up another crate and followed him.

As they left the cellar and their footsteps died away, it hit me that in all the confusion, Furze's mate had forgotten to tie me up.

Jimmy moaned. "They're going to get away with it!" He sounded anguished.

"Look!" I showed him my unbound hands.

Donna gasped. "Quick, untie us both and we've still got a chance to stop them."

I shook my head. Ever since I'd realised I wasn't a prisoner after all, my brain seemed to have been working at superhuman speed, suggesting and rejecting possible ways I could use my freedom to stop the thieves. Suddenly I knew what I had to do, but there was no time to untie the other two before Furze and his friend returned for the remainder of the wine.

"If they notice we're all gone when they come back, they'll be after us like a shot. If you stay here, with a bit of luck they won't realise there's only two of us left, especially with hardly any light to see by. I've got an idea. Trust me."

"But Alex…!" I heard Donna cry as I sped up the stairs. I ignored her. If my plan was going to work, there was no time to argue.

25

Showdown

I just made it across the hall to the living room before I heard the sound of two pairs of footsteps hurrying down the kitchen passage towards the hall. I hid behind the sofa again until the footsteps died away, then raced across the room and into the conservatory. I pushed past the towering potted plants and slipped out through the door into the garden. Then I ran along the back of the house until I reached the archway leading to the yard.

Cautiously, I poked my head around the side of the arch. The van was still parked in the yard, with the back doors open. It was already quite full of crates of wine. The Priory sweltered in the afternoon sun, and a white butterfly flew past my head and on into the yard, but otherwise there was no movement anywhere.

I was planning to disable the van, but to do that I needed to get some supplies from the kitchen. Because Furze and his mate would be coming back through the kitchen to get to the van, I needed to stay hidden until they had offloaded the next load of crates and returned for the last two. Then I would have only a few minutes to slip into the kitchen, find what I wanted, carry out my plan, and hide again before they returned with the final load.

In the meantime I tried not to think about what they might do to me if I was caught sabotaging their plans. My heart started racing every time I remembered the gun. And what if they had noticed I was gone and used the gun to frighten Donna and Jimmy into telling them where I was?

I was wondering whether I should abandon the whole plan as too dangerous when the two men came out of the kitchen door, laden with crates. The fat man was huffing and puffing with the effort of carrying the heavy weight, and after he had deposited the crate in the van, he leaned against the side of the vehicle, trying to catch his breath. Furze glared at him. "You can rest later. This is no time for a break!"

His mate scowled at him. "I agree. The sooner we're out of here, the better. Why didn't you tell me the place was haunted?"

As they went back indoors, I heard Furze reply. "It's not haunted, you fool. I told you, it's just those damn kids playing tricks."

I counted up to ten to allow them time to get back to the cellar before I raced over to the kitchen door. As I hurried through the scullery and into the kitchen, Boss Cat jumped down off his favourite chair and sidled up to me, rubbing himself against my legs. I brushed him away impatiently, and he stuck his tail in the air and stalked off, offended.

As usual, Mrs Liddell had left a bowl of fruit on the kitchen table, together with a big bottle of fizzy drink. I grabbed a banana from the bowl, and the bottle of fizz, and dashed back into the yard.

When the van had first driven into the yard, I'd noticed it was the same make that Granddad had used when he worked as a delivery man. On one occasion when I'd been curious about how the engine worked, Granddad had spent time explaining to me how petrol was converted into motion, and how the cooling and exhaust systems worked. Thanks to him, I knew exactly what I had to do to disable the van, and where to find the fuel inlet and the exhaust pipe.

Glancing round to make sure I was still alone, I knelt down by the rear of the van and reached underneath the chassis, desperately feeling for the end of the exhaust pipe. It only took a moment to locate it, and a few seconds more to stuff the banana firmly into the pipe. That should stop them in their tracks, but just in case it didn't I raced over to the fuel inlet and emptied the bottle of fizzy drink into the hole. I'd just finished when I heard raised voices coming from the kitchen. They were coming back, and there was absolutely nowhere in the yard for me to hide.

I panicked. My heart felt as if it was performing somersaults and my brain turned to cotton wool, so I couldn't think straight. Then there was a terrific yowl from the kitchen, followed by a loud crash, and the fat man swore loudly. The next minute Boss Cat streaked across the yard and disappeared into the garden. I guessed the fat man had tripped over the cat. As I grabbed the opportunity to run after Boss Cat through the archway and into the garden, I could hear raised voices from the kitchen.

As I leaned back against the stone arch where I was

safely hidden from view and tried to calm my racing heart, I heard the two men emerge into the yard. They were still arguing and Furze sounded absolutely furious. "First you allow all that supernatural mumbo-jumbo to get to you, and then you trip over the cat! You're a liability. I should never have involved you!"

"That's rich," I heard the fat man say. "If I hadn't pretended to be Prince Walid to give you a reference, you would never have got this job in the first place. You owe me!"

Furze ignored him. "I'm going to fetch my gear. Make sure the van's secure." I heard footsteps pounding up the steps to his flat, and then the sound of the van's doors being slammed shut.

It suddenly hit me that if Furze and his mate were going to be caught, I needed to phone the police urgently. There wasn't time to wait and see whether or not the van started. Furze had our mobiles, so I would have to use the landline in Mr Devlin's study. As quickly as my shaking legs would let me, I turned and ran round the back of the house and through the conservatory to the living room. So far there was no sound of the van starting up. I was rushing across the hall on my way to the study when there was a loud knock at the front door. It couldn't be the Devlins; they would have driven the car into the yard and gone into the house through the kitchen. So would Liddy and Parsons. Praying it would be someone who could help us, I pulled back the bolts and opened the door.

Standing in front of me was a tall young man with the same ginger hair as Jimmy, and a girl with very short blonde hair. "Hello," the young man said, staring at me. "Who are you?"

I'd never in my life been so glad to see anyone. "I'm Alex," I said. "But never mind that! Come inside, quickly. Furze is trying to steal your dad's wine collection, and Jimmy and Donna are tied up in the cellar."

Harry was brilliant. As soon as I explained the situation, and what I'd done to try and disable the van, he instantly took charge. First he phoned the police and told them a couple of armed men were trying to burgle the Priory. Then he gave his own set of keys to the girl so she could get into the cellar to free Jimmy and Donna. After that he and I rushed upstairs and looked out of the window at the end of the bedroom corridor, where we were safely out of sight of Furze and his mate but could see what was happening in the yard.

It was almost funny, watching them. Furze was beside himself. "You fool! Why didn't you check the van was roadworthy before you left?"

"You can talk!" the fat man replied. "You told me everybody was going to be out today. Got that wrong, didn't you?"

Then, just as it looked as if they might attack each other, we heard someone shouting. "This is the police! You are surrounded. Throw down your weapons and put your hands above your head."

Furze froze. He looked stunned. His mate leaned back against the van, breathing heavily, and for a moment I thought he was going to have a heart attack. Then both men raised their hands in the air. As armed policemen approached them from both directions, I heard Furze speak in a trembling voice. "The gun's in the van, but it's only a replica."

I gasped. "We spent hours feeling terrified, and it wasn't even a real gun!"

Harry patted me on the shoulder. "You weren't to know. We've got fake guns in our props department, and they look just like the real thing. Come on, let's go and find the others."

We went back downstairs and found Donna and Jimmy waiting for us in the hall with the girl, who I guessed was Harry's girlfriend. Jimmy raced over to Harry and gave him an enormous hug. Donna glared at me. "You might have untied us before running off like that!"

Before I could reply, Mr and Mrs Devlin walked in through the open front door. Jimmy's mum was looking distraught.

"What on earth is going on?" she asked. "There are armed police everywhere, and Furze is being taken away in handcuffs." Then she caught sight of Harry. "Oh, Harry!" she cried, and burst into tears.

26

A Confession

After that, there was so much going on that events became a bit of a blur. There seemed to be police officers everywhere, both inside the house and in the grounds. After a while, a plain-clothes detective arrived and told us all to go and wait in the living room so they could take statements from us. Jimmy's mum was still crying and Jimmy and Harry were trying to comfort her, while Mr Devlin had collapsed into an armchair, looking shell-shocked.

Donna and I sat together on the big squashy sofa. Donna was ignoring me, obviously still annoyed at me for leaving her tied up in the cellar. I was just relieved it was all over, and we hadn't got a huge ticking off from Mr Devlin for turning up at the Priory after he had banned us. Before the detective came back to take our statements, I whispered to Donna. "Shall we leave out all the supernatural stuff in the cellar?"

She gave me a frosty look, but nodded. "They'd never believe any of it, anyway."

When the detective finally returned, Mr Devlin roused himself. "I hope you have both men firmly under lock and key now."

The detective nodded. "Yes, sir. And we'll be charging them with attempted robbery and unlawful imprisonment of the children."

It took ages for the detective to take statements from everybody. When it was my turn I told him how stupid I felt for not realising the gun was a fake. He said the same thing as Harry. "We've confirmed he used to be an actor. It's an actor's job to make things look real, so it's no surprise you were taken in."

By the time he'd finished, the grandfather clock in the corner of the room was chiming six o'clock. Just then, one of the police officers came in and whispered in the detective's ear. He raised his eyebrows at Donna and me. "It seems I'd better let you two go home. Your grandmother has filed a missing persons report."

So much had happened that afternoon that we had forgotten all about Nan. Donna put her hand over her mouth. "Oh no! She'll never forgive us!"

The detective turned to the police officer who had brought the message. "See these two home safely, and explain to their grandmother what's been going on."

During the drive home in the police car, neither of us said a word, because we were both scared stiff about how Nan was going to react when we got back. As the constable escorted us up the front path, Nan appeared in the doorway. She looked thunderous.

The constable spoke before she could open her mouth. "Don't be too hard on them, Mrs Macintyre. They helped foil a major robbery. You should be proud you have two such resourceful grandchildren."

As the constable got back into his car, Nan was still

looking grim. Then, just as we were all about to go into the house, a taxi turned into our road. As it pulled up next to us, we saw a familiar face in the back seat.

"Dad!" Donna shrieked, dashing over to hug him as he emerged from the cab. "You're home a day early!"

Dad looked a bit overwhelmed at getting such an enthusiastic welcome, but you could tell he was pleased we had missed him. He was just explaining how he had managed to catch an earlier flight when he noticed the police car pulling away from the kerb and frowned. "What's happened, Mum? Why were the police here?"

Donna and I glanced at each other and I bit my lip. Dad sighed. "I knew it! You two have been in trouble again, haven't you? Let's go inside, so I can hear the bad news sitting down."

*

Early the following day, we got a phone call from Jimmy. "Can you come round now? There's something you need to hear. I'll ask Alf to pick you up."

We were glad to have an excuse to get out of the house. Things were still tense at home. We had told Dad and Nan how we had gone ghost-hunting, helped look for the missing ring, and then tried to stop Furze stealing the vintage wine, but we had been very careful not to mention the gun. Then Nan had turned on the television to watch the evening news, and the first item had screamed 'Armed robbery foiled at country house.' Nan had gone pale. "Armed? You mean they had guns?"

No matter how many times we pointed out that

the gun was a fake, it didn't make any difference. In the end, it was Dad who calmed Nan down. "I know they caused you a great deal of worry, Mum, disappearing like that, but I think you should give them some credit for wanting to help their friend, and using their initiative to try and stop the thieves." Then he looked sternly at us. "But I want your assurance that there will be no more messing with criminals in future. Is that understood?"

We promised, of course, but we both knew that we had only got off so lightly because Dad had come home in a good mood after a successful trip. Another time we mightn't be so lucky.

When we got out of the Rolls outside the Priory on Sunday morning, the house looked so peaceful that it was difficult to believe the whole place had been swarming with police only a few hours before. Then a first floor window opened, and Jimmy poked his head out. "Come on up," he called out. "We're all in my bedroom."

As we walked across the yard and entered the kitchen, I noticed that the van had disappeared. There was no sign of Mrs Liddell either, but Boss Cat was dozing on his favourite chair. He raised his head and stared at us sleepily as we passed him.

When we reached Jimmy's room, we found Jimmy had been joined by Harry and his girlfriend. I'd been too distracted to pay much attention to her the day before, but now that I was sitting right opposite her, I found her a bit scary. Her blonde hair was so short it could have been shaved by a barber, and she had a huge tattoo of a dragon down her left arm. She gave us a lazy, confident smile.

"Come on, Jimmy, introduce us!"

"Sorry!" Jimmy said. "Jo-Jo, this is Alex and Donna."

"Hiya." Jo-Jo said, then dug Harry in the ribs. "Your turn now, Hal."

Harry gave a rueful smile. "We have a confession to make," he said, "and we thought you two ought to hear it in person."

I looked at Jimmy. He had a huge grin on his face. "Harry told me the story last night. You're never going to believe this."

So we sat and listened while Harry told us how he had met Jo-Jo, who worked in the costume department at Vintage Films, and who knew Holcombe Bay because her aunt owned a caravan there. When Jo-Jo became his girlfriend, he told her about the Priory and how it was supposed to be haunted.

Jo-Jo nodded. "That was when I said – just as a joke, really – 'Wouldn't it be fun to try to pass ourselves off as ghostly monks?'"

"And I thought that was a brilliant idea," Harry said, grinning. "I was still angry with Dad for refusing to let me become an actor. I figured if I could be such a convincing ghost that people were genuinely scared, then maybe I could persuade Dad I had some talent after all. I still had my set of house keys, and I came up with this plan for us to hide in the attics at the Priory and just emerge from time to time, disguised as monks, to give people a fright. So Jo-Jo got hold of two monks' habits that were used in *The Poisoned Chalice*, and one Friday evening after work we hitched a lift down to Holcombe Bay. Only things didn't go according to plan."

I was beginning to get the picture now. "That must have been two weekends ago, when we had the sleepover. That was the first time anyone saw any ghostly monks."

Harry nodded. "We let ourselves in the back gate and made our way to the chapel, where we changed into the habits. We thought we'd see how the land lay that night, and then plan some stunt for the next day. There was nobody around as we went down the path to the house and in through the kitchen door to the scullery The idea was to get some food from the larder and then make our way to the attics using the priest's stair. Unfortunately Liddy was still in the kitchen, and she saw us and started screaming."

"Poor old Liddy!" Jimmy said. "Nobody believed her when she said she'd seen a ghost. Furze told her she was a liar, and Dad thought she'd been at the port."

"So it was you we saw when we came in from the garden after our ghost hunt?" Donna said.

Jo-Jo nodded. "We were having a second attempt at getting some food from the larder, because by that time we were ravenous. We'd left the door to the priest's stair open, so we just had time to disappear in there before you came and searched the scullery. I was laughing so much I was afraid you'd hear me through the wall."

Jimmy was looking annoyed. "Why didn't you tell me you had found the priest's stair, Harry? We could have had great fun with that."

Harry shrugged. "I only found it a few days before I left home."

"And then your mum saw one of you in the corridor

later that night," Donna said. "You certainly gave her a fright."

Harry looked a bit ashamed then. "I'm really sorry about that. I didn't mean to upset her. I was careless. I'd come down from the attic to use the toilet, and she suddenly came out of her bedroom. I couldn't get back to the attic, so I dashed downstairs and hid in the kitchen. It was lucky Dad tripped over Sir Hubert, or he might have found me."

"Liddy noticed there was food missing from the larder," Donna said. "She accused us of having a midnight feast."

"So you two were the hooded figures we caught sight of at the barbecue?" I asked.

Harry nodded. "Last weekend we came down again, but that time we borrowed the caravan from Jo-Jo's aunt, so we had somewhere to stay. We didn't know about the barbecue until we reached the gate on the cliff path and heard all the music. So we changed into the robes before letting ourselves into the garden, and hung around in the chapel trying to decide what to do. That was when that woman saw us and had hysterics. We left as quickly as we could after that."

Jimmy was looking puzzled. "What I'd really like to know is how you created all that supernatural stuff – the lights going on and off, the strange noises, the picture falling off the wall..."

Harry and Jo-Jo both looked blank.

"What are you talking about?" Harry said. "All we did was pretend to be ghostly monks. What else has been going on?"

Jimmy stared at Harry. "I don't believe you. Come on, you've been working for a film company. I bet you've learned lots about creating special effects."

Harry shook his head. "It wasn't us, honest! Are you telling me this place really *is* haunted?"

So then it was our turn to tell Harry and Jo-Jo about the lights that turned themselves on and off, the portrait of Major William Coverly that fell down of its own accord, and all the eerie things that had happened in the cellar. Jimmy showed Harry the book he'd found which told the story of the dead kitchen boy, and Donna explained how Emerald had sensed Seth's presence when she visited the Priory, and how she felt he had been trying to contact her in her dreams.

Talking about all the supernatural activity reminded me of something I wanted to ask Jimmy. "What happened to those letters on the wall in the cellar? Are they still there?"

Jimmy shook his head. "Soon after you left the cellar, they gradually started to fade, and by the time Jo-Jo came down to rescue us, they had disappeared. It was just as well they did; it would have been difficult explaining to the police how they got there."

Just then, Jimmy's dad stuck his head round the door, looking less confident than usual. "I wonder if you lot would mind coming downstairs. I've got something to tell you."

We all stood up and followed him down the stairs to the living room, where we found Jimmy's mum waiting for us. Mr Devlin sat down next to his wife and clasped her hand in his. He looked extremely nervous.

"What is it, Dad?" Jimmy asked.

Mr Devlin cleared his throat. "I'm afraid I've got some bad news. I'm very sorry, but we're going to have to leave the Priory."

27

Emerald Surprises Everyone

After Mr Devlin made his announcement, there was a stunned silence. Then Jimmy asked, "Why, Dad?"

Mr Devlin hung his head. "I'm so sorry," he said. "I've been a fool, and the only way I can sort things out now is to sell the Priory."

It turned out he had been encouraged by some of his wealthy new friends to make some unwise investments. Because he didn't really understand what he was doing, he had lost most of what was left of the lottery money. His financial affairs were now in such a mess that the only way he could repay his debts was to sell the house, the Rolls and the collection of vintage wines. When he'd finished his explanation, he turned to Jimmy's mum and started apologising all over again, but she cut him short. I couldn't help noticing that for the first time since we had known her, she actually looked cheerful.

"Oh, Ted! How could you think I'll miss this place? You know I've never been happy here. All I want is to go back to our old life at the bakery."

Mr Devlin looked astonished, then relieved. He turned to Jimmy. "How do you feel about this, Jimmy?"

Jimmy was beaming. "I just want us to be a happy

family again, like we were before. I don't care where we live."

Mr Devlin turned to Harry. "What about you, son?"

Harry shrugged. "I'm going to be living in London from now on, Dad. It doesn't matter to me where you're living when I come and visit you."

Jimmy's mum grasped her husband's hand more firmly. "The old bakery is still empty, isn't it? If there's any money left after selling everything, we could do up the shop and make a fresh start."

"And another thing, Dad," Harry said. "Don't you think Alex and Donna deserve a reward for stopping Furze stealing the wine?"

Mr Devlin, who seemed to have forgotten we were still there, clapped his hand to his forehead. "Of course! What am I thinking of?" He dug his hand in his jacket pocket and brought out a handful of money. Counting out five twenty-pound notes, he handed them to me. "Make the most of it. This may be the last time I'll be handing out large sums of money to anyone."

After we had thanked Jimmy's dad for the money, we said goodbye to Mr and Mrs Devlin, Harry and Jo-Jo and walked with Jimmy across the hall and out of the front door for the last time. We were going to go home via the cliff path and collect our bikes from the caravan park, where we had left them the day before. However, when we got outside we found a small van with *Holcombe Bay Echo* in big letters on the side had just drawn up in front of the house, and a man with a camera slung round his neck was getting out of the van. When he saw us, he smiled broadly.

"Just the guys I want to see. I want to hear all about how you thwarted those thieves yesterday, and don't spare the juicy details!"

★

On Monday morning, when the local paper dropped through the letterbox, the headline on the front page said '*Plucky teenagers foil robbery.*' Next to it was a big picture of the three of us standing in front of the Priory, and police mugshots of Furze and his mate.

When we got to school, we were immediately surrounded by kids wanting to hear the story all over again. We were still being bombarded with questions as the Pitbull arrived to take assembly. "QUIET!" he roared, and seemed to glare at us more ferociously than ever. But even the Pitbull couldn't stop me smiling that morning. Not only would he now have to revise his opinion of the Macintyres as a totally useless family, but we had also earned ourselves a hundred pounds for the second time in just a few months. As Donna pointed out as we made our way to our first class, "Now Eye Spy Investigations has had two successful cases, we're going to be everybody's first choice when there's a mystery to be solved."

Becoming local celebrities also helped to solve Donna's problems with Cat and Jasmin. We were now more popular than they were, and the next time they tried to make fun of Donna, Jason Dundy came to her rescue. "Give it a rest, you two," he told Cat and Jasmin. "You're getting boring." As a result, Donna was looking much happier. So was Jimmy, when Donna, Emerald and I finally caught up with him a few days later. He had lots of news.

"One of Dad's wealthy friends has offered to buy the wine collection as an investment, and another local bigwig wants to buy the Priory and the Rolls. We'll just keep the old family car that Mum drives. And Dad's offered to use any money he has left over to pay for Harry to go to drama school."

"What's happening to Liddy and Parsons when you leave?" Donna asked. "Are they going to work for the new owner?"

Jimmy grinned. "Alf may, but Liddy's already left. She was trying to tell Mum the 'right' way to do something, and Mum finally lost her temper and told her she was a bully and a rotten cook and the sooner she left the better. I wanted to clap. It's as if Mum's a different person now she knows she's leaving the Priory."

Emerald, who had been silent while Jimmy was talking, suddenly spoke up. "Has there been any more supernatural activity since the ghostly writing appeared in the cellar?"

Jimmy shook his head. "Everything's peaceful again. Sometimes it's difficult to believe any of it ever happened. It's as if the ghost boy has just gone away."

"Did your mum ever find her ring?" Emerald asked, changing the subject.

"No, and the detective said Furze swore he knew nothing about it."

Emerald nodded. "I think I know where it is," she said. "I don't think Furze took it after all."

We all stared at her.

"How can you know that?" Donna asked.

"Well…" Emerald blushed and bit her lip. She always hates being the centre of attention. Then she looked at me. "Remember I told you how I was getting all these strange dreams where the ghost boy was trying to speak to me?" I nodded. "Well, last night I had the dream again, and for the first time, I could hear what he was saying quite clearly. He told me that the ring was down the side of the seat in your mum's car, where she dropped it on the way back from the jeweller's."

Donna gasped. "Wow! You mean you actually spoke to a ghost? That's incredible!"

"Your mum needs to check the ring really is in the car, Jimmy," I pointed out. "Just in case the ghost got it wrong."

They all had a go at me then for still not believing one hundred per cent in ghosts after everything that had happened. When Jimmy texted us after school to say that his mum had found the ring exactly where the ghost boy said it would be, Donna threw me a triumphant glance. "Ready to believe now that ghosts really do exist?"

I shrugged. "Maybe. Or maybe not…"

I dodged out of the way as she threw a cushion at me.

A Note from the Author

Eye Spy II – Haunted is the second in a series of novels about Alex and Donna Macintyre and their detective service, Eye Spy Investigations.

I love hearing from readers, so if you would like to contact me, use the link on my website:
www.tessabuckley.com

And if you enjoyed reading this book, why not recommend it to your friends?